ADDICT

The Cassie Tam Files, Book 1

Matt Doyle

Published by
NineStar Press
PO Box 91792
Albuquerque, New Mexico, 87199
www.ninestarpress.com

Print ISBN #978-1-947139-04-6
Cover by Natasha Snow
Edited by Elizabeth Coldwell

New Hopeland was built to be the centre of the technological age, but like everywhere else, it has its dark side. Assassins, drug dealers and crooked businessmen form a vital part of the city's make-up, and sometimes, the police are in too deep themselves to be effective. But hey, there are always other options...

For P.I. Cassie Tam, business has been slow. So, when she's hired to investigate the death of a local VR addict named Eddie Redwood, she thinks it'll be easy money. All she has to do is prove to the deceased's sister Lori that the local P.D. were right to call it an accidental overdose. The more she digs though, the more things don't seem to sit right, and soon, Cassie finds herself knee deep in a murder investigation. But that's just the start of her problems.

When the case forces Cassie to make contact with her drug dealing ex-girlfriend, Charlie Goldman, she's left with a whole lot of long buried personal issues to deal with. Then there's her client. Lori Redwood is a Tech Shifter, someone who uses a metal exoskeleton to roleplay as an animal. Cassie isn't one to judge, but the Tech Shifting community has always left her a bit nervous. That wouldn't be a problem if Lori wasn't fast becoming the first person that she's been genuinely attracted to since splitting with Charlie. Oh, and then there's the small matter of the police wanting her to back off the case.

Easy money, huh? Yeah, right.

One

I ALWAYS DID like Venetian blinds. There's something quaint about them in a retro-tacky kinda way. Plus, they're pretty useful for sneaking a peek out the front of the building if I feel the need. That's something that you just can't do with the solid, immovable metal slats that come as a standard in buildings these days. That said, a thick sheet of steel is gonna offer you a damn sight more security than thin, bendable vinyl, so I keep mine installed. Just in case.

Another round of knocking rattles the front door, louder this time than the one that woke me.

The clock says 23:47, and the unfamiliar low-end car out front screams "Don't notice me, I'm not worth your time," which makes for the perfect combo to stir up the paranoia that the evening's beer and horror-film session left behind. This is my own fault. My adverts are pretty descriptive in terms of telling what I do: lost pets, cheating partners, theft, protection, retrieval of people and items, other odds and sods that the city's finest won't touch...I've got ways to deal with it all. That's right, I'm a real odd-job gal. The one thing that I don't put in there are business hours. The way I see it, even the missing pet cases usually leave me wandering the streets at half-past reasonable, so what's the point in asking people to call between certain hours?

More knocking, followed this time by the squeak of my letter box and a voice. "Hello? Cassandra Tam?"

It's funny, really. For all the tech advances that the world has made, no one has been able to improve upon the simple open-and-shut letter box. I stumble my way through the dark and wave dismissively at the frosted glass. The light switch and the keypad for the door lock are conveniently placed right next to each other on the wall to the right of the door, so *welcoming* my apparent guest is a nice, easy affair. The lock clicks a moment after the lights flood the room, and I pull the door open.

"Cassie," I say, turning and skulking my way back into the room. "Or Caz. Drop the Tam."

I hear a sniff behind me, and the lady from the letter box asks, "Are you drunk?"

"If I pass out in the next five minutes, then yes," I reply, turning the kettle on. I'd left it full, ready for the morning, but I guess this is close enough. "Take a seat at the table. Would you prefer tea or coffee? I'd offer beer, but since I reek of it, I guess I must've finished it."

Footsteps creep unapologetically across the room, and a chair squeaks on the floor. Good. If you can't deal with a snarky response to something, don't say it all, and if you *can* deal with it, then as far as I'm concerned you don't need to apologise.

"Coffee," the lady says. "So, do you always see potential clients in your underwear, or is it just my lucky day?" Her voice has a slightly playful edge to it, but with a sarcastic kick to round it off.

The business portion of my apartment comprises entirely of a small open-plan room separating my kitchen from my living room. And by open plan, I mean an allotted space that encroaches on both territories but is conveniently large enough to house what I need. Or, in other words, a table, four chairs, and nothing else. Since filing went near entirely digital, filing cabinets have pretty much become obsolete, so the two that I found dumped outside the building when I bought the place currently live in my bedroom, and contain a mix of quick access work stuff and personal files I'd rather not have floating on the net. Most things, though, I store electronically, the same as everything else.

I rarely use the business table to eat, read, or any of that junk, so until this evening it's been entirely empty for a good few weeks. The lady sitting there now is studying me, I can see, and probably wondering if this was a mistake. Whatever she may have expected, a Chinese-Canadian gal of average height in a cami top and a loose pair of sleep shorts most likely wasn't it. For what it's worth, though, I'm studying her just the same. She's a lithe-looking thing, dressed in a casual pair of jeans and a plain black fitted top under a leather jacket. If the metal plugs running down her shaven head like a shiny, rubber-tipped Mohawk weren't a giveaway for what she is, the light scarring punctuating the outer edges of her pale blue eyes certainly would be. She's a Tech Shifter, and like most of her ilk, she looks like a punk rocker gone cyborg.

"Only when people come calling near midnight," I say, crossing my arms. "And what about you? Do you have to work to rile people up, or is it just a talent?" I spot her wince and can't quite contain the smile that fights its way up to my lips. I can't really afford to lose another client, though, so I throw in another dismissive wave and add, "Don't worry about it. It's late, and I'm grumpy. Milk and sugar?"

She nods. "Two sugars, lots of milk, thanks."

I finish making the drinks and plonk myself into the chair opposite my guest. "So how about we start with a name?"

"Lori. Lori Redwood. And I'm sorry about calling so late, it's just that I didn't really know when would be best, and I figured that you probably wouldn't be busy this time of night."

"And whatever problem you have has been eating away at you, so you wanted to sort it as soon, eh?"

Lori nods and takes a gulp of her coffee. "Something like that."

I tilt my head, and rest my elbows on the table, letting my chin fall into my clasped hands. "I'm guessing this isn't a missing pet case?"

"No. Do you read the morning news sites?"

"I browse. Why?"

"Did you see any of the articles about Edward Redwood? They would have been late last week."

I close my eyes and cast my mind back to the things I'd read over the last couple of days. The name is familiar, and not just because of the articles, but I can't place where from.

"Virtual Junkie, died of an accidental overdose of synthesised stimulants?" I try.

Lori nods again. "He was my brother. It wasn't an accidental OD, though."

I sigh. "I'm sorry for your loss, but he was an Addict, right? That's what the press said. He wouldn't be the first VJ Addict to OD, and he won't be the last."

"You don't understand. Yes, Eddie was an Addict, but he couldn't have overdosed himself, because he never used stimulants. He used to make a really big deal out of how he preferred the experience pure, because he didn't want to mess up his chances of becoming a Pro."

I shake my head sadly. "Miss Redwood..."

"Lori, please," she cuts in.

"Lori, then. Let me give you a history lesson. Many years ago, some bright spark realised society had become so reliant on electronic tools that most jobs carried out by big businesses could be done virtually. As things advanced, they built a whole virtual world where people could work, and gradually, the staff who pulled the long shifts became reliant on the feel of being in the place. Meanwhile, out in the real world, regular people accessed the virtual world to communicate with the staff, and to play games, and they too became reliant on the feel of the place. And so, two types of Junkie were born; the Pros, supported by their bosses, and the Addicts, who were no different to the drug users of the twentieth century. Now don't get me wrong, I'm not judging anyone here, but Addicts don't become Pros. Both types of VJ get unhealthily hooked, but the Addicts don't have the support to keep it in check. They *all* end up on the stimulants eventually."

"Not Eddie," she insists. "He had a contract lined up. All he had to do was pass the entrance test, and he'd transition to Pro."

"Now that's a first. Who with?"

"I don't know. That's part of the problem."

I narrow my eyes. "Lori, why exactly did you come to me?"

"Because the police won't reopen the case. They said there's no evidence that anyone else was in the room at all when he died. If I can just figure out who he was negotiating with, then that would be something."

"So, what? You want me to find out who your brother was supposedly going to be hired by?"

"Yes."

"And then what?"

"I find out how he ended up OD-ing on something that he wouldn't touch, and why."

I down my coffee and lean back in my chair, crossing my arms again. "You think that he was murdered, don't you? By someone in whatever company he was supposedly talking to."

"Yes," she replies vehemently, then shrinks back a little and adds, "I don't know. Maybe. It's the only thing that makes sense, right?"

"No, it's not. What makes the most sense is that your brother was no different from any other VJ Addict, and he just hid his usage from you. Let's say for one moment we can even entertain the idea that a Pro company were willing to hire an Addict. That isn't even close to a strong enough link to start crying murder. Honestly, Lori, I get it, but you're reaching here. You're trying to grasp onto anything that can make this all easier for you, and that's fine. But trust me on this. No amount of grasping at nothing ever changes anything."

Lori has clearly been fighting back the tears, and my little speech just pushed her over the edge. She wipes her eyes on her sleeve and gets to her feet, keeping her head hung low.

"I'm sorry to bother you," she says, and turns back towards the door. "I'll see myself out."

"Where are you going?" I ask.

"Home."

"Why?"

"To look up some more names. You've made your position quite clear."

"I never said that I wouldn't take the case. I just wanted you to understand how unlikely your scenario is."

Lori stops in her tracks and looks back at me. "You'll do it?" she asks, her voice a conflicted mess of desperation and disbelief.

"If there's something to be found, then I'll find it."

"I...thank you. Thank you."

"Yeah, well, don't thank me yet," I reply, getting to my feet. I walk back to the kitchen, slide open one of the drawers, and pull out a small metal disc about one inch thick, and five inches in diameter. I throw it to Lori, and she whips her arm out, snatching it from the air. She turns it over in her hand, studying the glass top. "You seen one of those before?"

Lori shakes her head.

"It's a standard Case Tool, at least for me. Take it with you, and when you get home, tap the screen three times quickly. It'll load a bunch of files for you to complete. Don't worry, it comes with a holo-keypad, so you won't need to hook it up to anything. I prefer to keep things connected to *my* server, and mine alone when I can help it. Take your time, answer the questions with as much detail as possible, and tap to send them back to me. Before it'll send 'em, it'll ask you to enter your details to transfer the deposit for the case."

"Okay," she nods. "How much am I looking at?"

"Aside from being a potential murder case, this is gonna prevent me from taking on any other work for the duration, so I'm not gonna be working cheap. The deposit's five thou. If I find nothing, that'll be it, but if something turns up, I'll expect the same again on completion. That cool?"

"Yes. Absolutely. Thank you."

"Not a problem. Now get yourself home so that I can get some sleep."

Two

MY ALARM KICKS in at 06:30, pulling me out of what I'm pretty sure is too little sleep for my line of work. I'm not in the least bit surprised to see the red light flashing silently on the metal disc by the clock, signalling that it's received the files from its sister piece. There's no way to tell what time they were sent without opening the files, but given Lori's resolution that her brother didn't OD, I'd guess a couple of hours after our meeting is a safe bet.

I sit up with a yawn and stretch my arms high behind my head, working out the shoulder kinks that I develop most nights. I guess it's nearing time to change the mattress again. Shame, that. This one's seen me through more than its fair share of lonely nights, cowering from the imaginary monsters on the TV screen. All things considered, I've gotten myself into enough life-or-death situations that crappy gore fests and jump scares shouldn't really affect me, but somehow, they do. Every time. In fact, I'm pretty sure that I was at the start of a nightmare when Lori woke me up last night.

In a way, I'm surprised that the nightmares didn't come again after speaking with her. That happens sometimes when I've been talking with Tech Shifters. I think they just remind me how close we are to creating our own monsters like the ones that we see in the movies. Tech Shifters have only really been around for about five years now, and when the call went out for volunteers to test the prototypes, it was initially answered by the three Fs: Furries, Fetishists, and Freaks.

The Furs were harmless enough. For the most part, they were just an internet fandom that, thanks to modern advancements, got to live out their dream of shifting into whatever animal they felt close to. Very few of the group were interested, or so I heard, but those that were, were happy enough to be identified by their social clique. The Fetishists never caused any trouble either. For them, metal exo-suits just became an alternative to leather and PVC. It was the Freaks that caused the problems. They were the unstable ones who had enough sense to hide their demons. Within a month of the project going live, we had modern-day werewolves running around tearing people's throats out and howling at the moon. It was a good time for business. I got to moonlight with the city's finest for a few cases, and that meant a flat rate of pay for the duration, but the messes that we had to wade through, sometimes literally, were more than enough to make me distrusting of the Tech Shifter community for a few years after.

These days, things are better controlled. You want the plugs, you gotta pass a full pre-op psych test first. Even the law enforcement industry is getting in on it now that the tech's bedded in better. Hell, the local PD has its own TS Division with five full-time operatives; three hybrid shifters and two full animals. And the national army? Well, they've got a whole lot more than that.

People still remember those early nights of being afraid to walk the streets during the full moon, though, and their memories don't often differentiate between the F types, let alone the ever-growing legion of Cs—the Curious and the Casual. Why anyone would take body-modding that far without a serious affinity for what they're doing is beyond me, but that's humans for you. I wonder which grouping Lori fits into? Here's hoping she's not a Third F that slipped the net.

Looking at the dressing gown hanging limply from the end of the bed, I'm beginning to wonder why I didn't grab it before answering the door last night. Beer is probably the answer to that. In my experience, it's the answer to most things. Even then, though, I would have probably gone back to get it if Lori hadn't mentioned what I was barely wearing. Challenge me and woe betide you if you think I'm changing a damn thing. Stubbornness is my oldest friend, and if he thinks that you're trying to pick a fight, he'll come out to play every time. There aren't any challengers around now, though, so I grab the gown and slip it on, then chuck the disc into one of the pockets and head to the kitchen.

The kettle boils nice and quickly, and I fill a mug with black coffee. I screw my face up and make a disgusted grunt after the first mouthful. Black coffee sucks, but unfortunately, it's needed if I'm to survive the morning without passing out.

"Let's see what we've got," I grunt, and slip the disc onto the business table.

AND SO I came to snort and grumble my way through the written ramblings of my first paying client in over a month. To her credit, Lori has clearly given me as much as she can in terms of details. Unfortunately, word count does not equal actual content, so that doesn't equate to much more than she gave me last night. It sounds cold, but the fact that she was the one who found his body makes no difference in the grand scheme of things. The description of the room will give me something to get started with, but without knowledge of whether anything she's described is out of the ordinary, I don't have the context to make much out of it. What I really need was the name of his dealer. Of course, she wouldn't know that, though. She doesn't have the jittery eyes of a user herself, and she honestly believes that the dearly departed Eddie Redwood was the one exception to the rule of VJ Addict behaviour.

I pick up my elderly tablet and hold the power button until it starts to join me in the waking word. "Good...morning, Cassandra," it says, failing again to connect to the network at the speed it used to when I bought it. I tap the voice command button and it asks, "How may I be of assistance?"

"Local web search," I say, speaking slowly. "Search term, Edward Redwood. Timeframe, last two weeks. Sort newest first."

After an excruciating seven seconds, the screen flickers and I get my first run of results. The articles are pretty short, with the most recent ones reciting the official decision by the investigating officer, Corporal Devereux. That it was assigned to a corporal rather than a specialist division speaks volumes about how seriously the police took the case. What that means is there weren't any immediate signs that it was anything other than what they said it was: an accidental OD.

The local PD get progressively more corrupt the higher you go, but the lower ranks are still the good guys here. Mostly. The reports say that Eddie's body contained traces of Flash7, enough to suggest he took a three hundred milligram dose. The level's high, but the drug isn't unusual. So far, so ordinary.

The next chunk of reports deal with the discovery of the body. There's nothing really there that Lori hasn't told me in her files. I note that all the reports use the same photo of the body, all of which are copyrighted to...Lori Redwood. She must be a freelance photographer. Either she drew the short straw in having to photo the scene for the press, or she wanted to do it herself rather than let someone else in to something so close to home.

The other hits relate to a different Eddie Redwood, a botanist who was touring through town to demonstrate some sort of synthetic solar-powered earth.

Okay then, let's change tack. Time to see if I can figure out where I know his name from. I'm pretty sure that it's from an old case file, but I couldn't say which one. I swipe the internet away and tap the voice command button again.

"How may I be of assistance?" the tablet asks.

"Document content search, target, case files. Search term Edward Redwood or Eddie Redwood."

A big green circle starts spinning on the screen, and I chuck the tablet onto the table and head back to the kitchen. Cup of coffee number two, milky this time, comes with some stale bread and jam. By the time I've finished the drink, the circle is still swirling merrily around, and the completion percentage has barely hit 20 percent. I sigh and swipe down the top bar, then tap the local system icon.

Within moments, a voice cuts through the room speakers. "Synch to local system complete. Please state your desired settings."

"Single room audio. Tracking mode target, Cassandra Tam."

A beep, then, "Settings active."

I nod in thanks, knowing full well that my internal system isn't even close to being an AI, and take myself off to the bathroom.

Three

MY SHOWER IS an old-style cubicle with a manual control system that cost far more to install than it was worth. Hey, it's my apartment; I can do what I want with the place. My shower is like my blinds; it's a personal preference born from specific necessities. In this case, that necessity stems from my distrust for a computer to get the right temperature. It's the same reason I disabled the automatic feature on the central heating and air con, and why I have a near-antique kettle that needs repairing every three to four months. The way I see it, tech is good for some things, like saving me from having to search through hundreds of case files manually, or providing a decent equaliser during confrontations, but when it comes to temperatures? Nuh-uh. Computers don't even use cooling fans since stuff went solid-state, so what the hell do *they* know about comfortable temperatures?

I close my eyes and point my face straight up into the stream of water, letting the warm spray wash away the last traces of sleep and plaster my hair to my back, darkening the strands from mousy auburn to black. My father was the son of the son of the son of an immigrant, and the first of his line to marry outside what my grandfather referred to as *our culture*. Genetics being what they are, the result of this is that my skin tone, like my hair, is my father's, but lightened slightly by my mother's Canadian heritage.

If a God truly designed me, he must have liked to mix and match like that, 'cause he kept it going until he was done. My father's untoned and slightly bulkier-than-I'd-like mass lays awkwardly on my mother's delicate hips and tidy breasts. His slightly crooked teeth and Chow-Yun Fat smile sits behind her full lips. His strength plays off her flexibility of movement. His masculine hands and feet, her naturally shiny nails.

I always found it ironic that everything that I inherited from my mother had a softening effect on my appearance, when my father was by far the softer of the two in terms of personality. I loved them both for that. My father's quiet determination was something to be admired, and my mother's constant stream of foul-mouthed tirades made her seem hilarious to me and friends back when I was in school. We were a mixed-up little family that somehow worked, and I sat there in the middle, "a perfect representation of the balance between us." Or that's what my father called me anyway. Looking back on it and how we all were, it makes me glad that I grew up in Vancouver, where the people judged you less for how you looked and more for what you could do. Or most did, anyway.

But that life is gone now, and that's *my* fault.

"Search complete," the room speakers say.

I turn my head away from the shower spray and reply, "Summarise hit numbers."

"Search term, Edward Redwood. Zero complete matches, one partial match. Search term, Eddie Redwood. Zero complete matches, one partial match."

"Are both partial matches the same?"

"Checking...complete. Confirmed, individual partial match applies to both searches."

I flick the dial back around to zero, and the shower cuts out abruptly, the warm hiss immediately replaced with the light *put-put* of the water dripping off my back while I reach around the steamed-up door and clamber for a towel.

"Summarise file details."

"Client: Tobias Martin. File category: Financial Irregularities. Subcategory: Theft."

I step out of the shower and start heading towards the bedroom, rubbing my hair ferociously with the towel. Tobias Martin. That was about six months ago. "Summarise partial hit."

"Audio transcript two, lines two hundred and ninety-seven to two hundred and ninety-eight. Shall I search for the audio file?"

I only record interviews if there's going to be a lot to discuss that either I or the police may need to refer to later. The audio file will likely be pretty large, though, and leaving my tablet to scan it for the right lines is just asking for another hour of doing nothing. Tempting, but no.

"No, just read it."

"Tobias Martin states, 'There's Lori Redwood, she's like our Alpha, but it wouldn't be her.' End of match."

That's right, he was a Tech Shifter, second F. Money was mysteriously leaving his account in small but regular drips, and he couldn't figure out where it had gone or who had authorised the transfers because of some convoluted proxy system.

"Alpha, huh," I mumble. I drop the towel over my head like a hood and split two of the blinds with my middle and index fingers. The view outside says that it's gonna be a hot day, so I decide to quit scrubbing and let the sun do most of the work for me. I remember the Tobias Martin case well enough to know that I don't need to look into Lori in any great detail. Despite Tobias's assertions, I would have likely checked out any public records on her, but I wouldn't save those unless it looked like she was likely to be involved. I have a vague recollection of seeing a photo of her wearing pretty much the same outfit as she had when she came visiting, which means that the familiarity with the name was just a coincidence helped by a half-remembered photo.

Shame, that. That's one potential lead down.

Four

FOR LEGAL PURPOSES, I'm registered as a private investigator. The law of the land means that's enough to get me certain dispensations for my work, providing I follow procedure and fill out reams of digital paperwork before I go doing anything stupid. Sometimes, I don't bother.

You see, for the most part, I keep my nose clean and do things by the book. When I started up in this place, I made damn sure that I did everything the *right* way, rather than the way that gets quick results, and that let me get my foot in the door with the local PD. A couple of cases along, and I was known well enough that I was trusted by the ones who do their jobs because it's their job, if not the ones who only do the jobs that push them up the pay scale. There was a good reason to do things this way. My father taught me that if you want to get by as a PI, then you don't need friends in high places, you just need them in *high enough* places. You get that, and certain things can be filed retroactively if you get the right results.

The six-foot slab of moustache and middle-aged spread that is Captain Andrew Hoover cocks his head at me as he walks by, and brings himself to a stop at the desk where I'm scribbling some rough notes on a stupidly cumbersome web-based warrant application form with an oversensitive e-pen.

"White shirt, black tie and trousers, well-polished shoes...I'm half expecting to see you in a trench coat and a fedora one of these days."

"And hide all this from the world?" I grumble unenthusiastically, waving my pen hand roughly in the direction of my body. "Sounds too much like a crime to me."

Hoover laughs. "Someone's grouchy this morning. Must be a fun one you've gotten lumbered with."

"If only. You know of the Eddie Redwood case?"

Hoover slides a chair up and drops himself into it. He rests his elbow on the table and strokes his moustache like a pet. "Addict, right? OD'd on stimulants?"

"His sister doesn't think so. She said that you guys weren't interested in reopening the case for her, so she came to me instead. And who's Corporal Devereux, by the way?"

"New kid, transferred in from your end of town."

"Hollywood North, eh?" I reply, intentionally exaggerating the light Canadian lilt that still lingers in my voice.

"Yeah. He's a coupla years younger than you, though, not long out of the academy, so I doubt you know him. I'll introduce you next time he's around Wouldn't want him trying to block you on anything unnecessarily."

"Appreciated. So, do you think he missed anything, or am I chasing my tail here?"

Hoover crosses his arms behind his head and relaxes into a smile. "Keep barking, little doggy. I can't go into specifics, obviously, but no. It seemed pretty open and shut to me, I'm afraid, so you're gonna be running in circles for a while with this one."

"Great," I grunt.

"So who're the warrants for? Sanders said you asked for three of 'em."

"I'm leaving them blank for now. I'm gonna try stirring up an Addict Nest, see if I can get the names of some dealers. If I can prove that Eddie bought the stuff, that should be enough to close this off. If any of them don't play ball, I'll slap the warrant on them."

"You got a Nest in mind?"

"Nope. Sanders reckons he can find one for me before I'm done, though."

"I don't doubt it," Hoover replies, getting to his feet. "Just make sure you put the names on the form and send them off before you start hitting people this time."

"Yeah, yeah," I say, smiling to myself about the memory of a deserving prick who suddenly found himself with a bloody mouth.

Five

WAY BACK, NEW Hopeland used to be a tourist city. By that, people meant that the number of tourists entering the place every year was higher than the number of permanent residents. Built over part of Utah's Great Salt Lake Desert at the dawn of our current tech-enlightened age, it was the first new city built with a focus on utilising and progressing modern tech in everyday living. These days, near everywhere comes with the stuff built into every home as standard, but back then, it was an oddity right out of cheap sci-fi novels. Combine that with the optimistic name chosen to represent how forward thinking the country was becoming with this stuff, and you had a marketer's dream. Once the place was up and running, people flocked here for years.

These days, there's still a lot of people passing through, but those that visit tend to stay a lot longer. It's less a city for short-term visits now, and more a good place to go when you're running. Now that the rest of the country's converted to similar styles, it no longer gets the same attention from the rest of the world. It's small compared to the tech-enhanced metropoles of the day, but there are still plenty of big businesses here that are always looking to hire, and no one tends to ask too many questions. Unless you draw attention to yourself.

The three people behind the dented door in front of me have been drawing a lot of attention to themselves. Virtual Junkie Professionals work shifts that run nonstop and can last as long as three weeks. In return for their time, they get a helluva lot of support from their bosses. The chairs are well-built and comfy, the virtual-touch-sensitive gloves are cleaned heavily before every shift, and the workers are kept hydrated and sustained via drips while they work in their semiconscious state. The pay ain't bad either, or so I hear.

Addicts like Jim and Barbara Holland and their cousin Mark Farlow don't have the same type of lifestyle. They tend to use refurbed or homebrew equipment, jack themselves up on stimulants that increase feeling in the virtual world, and don't use drips. Instead of long-term shifts doing something useful, they usually run in groups and hang out in run-down little places like this, sharing one virtual profile that they take it in turns to use, one or two days at a time. With the way the headgear works, that leaves shared users with two choices: break the programming after each run so that it will accept the next person's retinal scan, or use an old-style model with the retinal scan disabled.

In truth, though, Addicts are useful. Pros are usually more than happy to help with any sort of investigation, but they're wrapped in so much red tape that it can take weeks before you can even begin to question them. Addicts take a little more convincing to cooperate, but once you crack them, they work quickly, if for no other reason than to get you out of their hair.

I give the door a quick rap with my knuckles, and when that doesn't get a response, I follow up with a series of hard kicks.

Finally, someone slaps the door from the other side and a jittery voice asks, "You got the password?"

"No, but I've got a warrant."

"Ah, fuck, man," the voice moans, and a series of locks start to click open one by one. The door slides heavily to the side, and an overly skinny man in a dirty vest top stumbles into the gap. He looks me up and down with his sunken eyes and says, "Let's see it, then."

"See what?"

"The warrant, man, the warrant," he groans, and his left arm starts to twitch, swinging up and slapping his right just above the elbow. The movement makes it look like he's swatting at some invisible fly. The way he smells, he could very well be attracting real ones.

I shove past him and step into the apartment. "I never said the warrant was for you," I tell him, and head down the hallway and into an open-plan room disappointingly similar to my own, but marginally less clean. In what was probably designed to be a living room, there's nothing but a large homemade log-in chair that looks like an eggshell cut top to bottom. Deep in the seat, an emaciated woman that I'm assuming is Barbara Holland shivers and smiles dreamily from under her headset.

Over in the kitchen at the other side of the room, another man sits at a small table, idly rolling an empty syringe from side to side. Unlike the guy at the door, he looks a little healthier, and is wearing a clean T-shirt and a pair of shorts. I'm guessing he's either the only one of the three with a job, or he just hasn't been using as long as they have.

"Hey! Hey, you can't be in here, man," the first man shouts, creeping his way into the room behind me and using the wall to keep himself upright.

The man at the table glances towards the other guy, then spots me. His head tilts slowly, looking me up and down. He smiles widely and says, "Tits an' tie. Nice."

"Sure they are," I reply. "Play ball, and I'll let you touch the tie."

"You listening to me, man," the first guy says, stumbling forward and gripping my shoulder as tightly as he can. "I said you can't be in here. Not without a warrant."

"This is a nice shirt," I reply. "I'd rather you didn't get it dirty."

"Come on, Jimmy boy," the man at the table laughs. "Be nice. We don't get many guests." He nods at me, and says, "Come, sit down."

I swat Jim Holland's hand away from my shoulder and stroll across the room, taking the only free chair. "Mark Farlow, I assume."

"The one an' only," he replies. "An' you are?"

"Cassandra Tam, PI."

"Ooh, a detective," he slurs, his tongue flicking sleazily over his dry, cracked lips. "An' what can we do for you, hmm?"

"I'm looking for some information. Do you know about the Eddie Redwood case?"

Mark raises his eyebrows curiously, but his eyelids droop slightly, betraying his tiredness. "Just another brother down. Shit like that happens when you fly solo, Detective. That's why we run as a three. Family lookin' out for family an' all that. I never met Eddie myself, wouldn't know him from any other faceless guy out there, but chances are, the police already called it for what it was."

"My client doesn't think so."

"An' you believe them?"

"No."

"Then why come here, interruptin' our fun, hmm?"

I cross my arms and fix Mark with a solid stare. "'Cause a paying client is a paying client. Either I prove the police were right, or I find something they missed. Either way, I give my client closure and get my money."

"Mercenary, ain't she?" Jim babbles from over by Barbara.

"We all gotta get our kicks somewhere," I say. "Like I said, all I want is some information. You give me that, and I'll let you get back to your *fun*."

"An' what information would you be wantin', Detective?" Mark replies.

"I need the names and addresses for the local dealers that have been active in the last month."

Mark's body tenses for the conflict that he knows is now coming, and he shakes his head stiffly. "No can do. We don't give up our own, not to the law."

I shoot Mark a dark smile. "Let me make this clear. As far as the police are concerned, they've got nothing to lose by letting me loose on this. Hell, it was them that gave me your details, Mr. Farlow. You see, if I prove them right, then my client stops harassing them. If I prove them wrong, then they're grateful to have another piece of scum off the street. It's a win-win situation for them. What that means is they'll let certain things slide if I get them a result at the end of it."

"Threats," Jim babbles. "That ain't right, man. You can't be here. Like I said, man, you can't be here."

"Jimmy boy, shut up, man," Mark growls, keeping his attention on me. "What exactly do you think you're gonna do to us, hmm? Look around you, Detective. I count two of us awake, an' one more that we can pull out of the net if we need to. You're just one chick runnin' her mouth."

"Running her mouth from those big ol' lips, man. She can't be here. She needs to get gone, man, gone."

I ignore Jimmy's cackling and pull my phone out of my pocket. Keeping my body angled squarely towards Mark, I drop my gaze to the screen and load up a photograph, then place the handset on the table. Mark's eyes twitch down at the display, then back up to me.

The corners of his mouth creep up into a victorious grin, and he says, "I see what you're doin'. Your phone's, what, six years old? You can show me all the pretty pictures you want. If you can't afford a decent handset, there ain't no way you got one of *those*."

The picture is a promo shot of a Familiar, an AI designed for mass production and wholesale. Like most Familiars, this one's fairly small, only about the size of my head. The vast majority of units are labelled as "Family Class" and function as pets. They're great with kids, or so I hear, and a bit sturdier than regular animals, but mostly they're just expensive status symbols. This particular one, though, is primarily a "Protector Class" unit. That means it rushes in like an attack dog, protecting its master with the ferocity of a twister in a shanty town. It's a pretty little thing, built to look like a beaked gargoyle with bat wings and steel-plated armour. The glint on the tips of the beak, wings, talons, and claws make it clear what its primary weapons are.

"Tell me, Mr. Farlow, do you know who Jonah Burrell is?"

"CEO of FE Ltd. What about him?"

"About a year ago, his daughter went missing..."

"Yeah, yeah," he cuts in. "Turned out she'd faked her kidnapping to run away with her lover. Daddy dragged her home in disgrace after he proved that the guy had been using her to try to buy a majority shareholding. What about him?"

"You're right. There's no way that I could afford a Familiar Unit on my earnings. But ol' Jonah was real grateful when I handed him my report. If the CEO of Familiar Enterprises feels like he owes you, how do you think he'd repay you?"

Mark narrows his eyes. "What did you say your name was?"

"Cassandra Tam."

"Yo, Jimmy, look it up."

I keep my face impassive, my gaze locked on Mark's while Jimmy mutters to himself and taps away at a tablet. Judging by the nervous drumming of his fingers, time must be creeping by at a crawl for Mark right now. Me, though? I'm enjoying it.

After a while, Jim stumbles over and drops his tablet down in front of Mark. "It's her, man. News report's got a picture and everything."

Mark doesn't even bother to look at the screen. He just keeps his attention fixed on mine. "You're bluffing," he states, the barest quaver sneaking up on the last word.

I give three short sharp whistles, and a window in one of the side rooms shatters, bringing Mark to his feet. The door to the right of the entrance hallway cracks open, and the thing from the photograph ambles arrogantly into the room, the last few shards of glass still sliding from its body while it shakes its wings. It clambers smoothly up the table leg, hops up onto my shoulder, and lets out a triumphant mechanical *caw*.

"I call him Bert," I say, using one finger to rub him under his chin. "He's been staying at FE Ltd.'s offices for his yearly servicing. I needed to pick him up today anyway, so I figured, why not take him on a little trip." I smile. "Now. How much damage do you think he can do to all your equipment?"

Six

VJ DEALERS HAVE this weird sort of underground unionisation going on. A lot of them hold down perfectly respectable day jobs, then deal in synth stimulants on the side. The way it works is that they all operate from the same stockpile, then run shifts where a handful of people do production, a few others do the selling, and the others take a break. At the end of the month, the sellers get to keep 30 percent of their takings, another 30 percent goes to the production team, and the remaining 40 percent gets split between those on a break and a central pot for buying supplies and funding the team when sales are down.

What they're doing isn't entirely legal, but the police stay out of their business most of the time. Aside from having far bigger fish to fry, there are a fair few casual users higher up in the chain of command, and this place is a hotbed for cross-country sales when certain members of the PD travel in for whatever pointless inspections they want to use as an excuse this time.

The good thing about that is it makes my job here a lot easier. After telling Bert to stick close but only come if I call, I cleared the first two dealers in under an hour. I'd already figured that they wouldn't turn out to be the ones to sell the stuff to the dearly departed Eddie. They were both at the smaller end of things, so their stock had been limited all month. But hey, all leads are worth checking. For all I knew, he could have gone to both and run two smaller transactions, or he could have bought multiple times.

Turns out he didn't. These two, one guy called Joe and one idiot calling himself L3G3ND, complete with threes replacing the e's, were more than happy to talk. Turns out they'd been paranoid that the police were gonna come knocking after they read about Eddie's death, and wanted to be sure that they could prove they didn't sell him the stuff that killed him. They even gave me lists of their sales to look at. Like I said, I wasn't expecting much from either of them, but I took photos of the lists anyway, just in case. I think that my visit came as a relief to them.

This next one was where I expected to find my proof. Charlotte Goldman, or Charlie for short, has been dealing for a long, long time, and I've spoken with her before when the need's arisen. Sometimes I come across people in my line of work and, depending on why I came into contact with them in the first place, we keep in touch in one way or another. When it comes to Charlie, I keep it to a "when I need to" basis, without exception. Or I do these days anyway, or else I would have been tempted to go straight to her for information rather than harassing Mark Farlow and his cousins.

The problem with not driving is that, unless I can solve something quickly, I end up walking all over the place, and leave myself tired and grumpy by the time I get near the end of the day. When I'm making a trip that I don't want to, it's worse. Luck has kept me from straying too far from the city centre thus far today, but I'm hardly cheery by the time I make it to Charlie's house on Fenchurch Street. Finding her standing in the doorway, waiting for me with that Cheshire cat smile of hers, doesn't help either.

"Caz!" she calls. "Still no car, huh? Come on in, I've got the coffee all ready to go."

"Great," I grumble to myself, and consider calling Bert down to wipe the annoying bounce from her voice.

"Joe called to say that you'd be visiting. He said that you'd been to see L3G3ND too, asking about Eddie Redwood?"

"That's right," I reply, sinking into one of her comfortable armchairs. She hands me a full mug, and I nod in thanks, take a gulp, and try to ignore both the burning sensation in my throat and my annoyance at how well she remembers how I like my coffee. I can't even remember how many sugars she takes now.

"So how are things?" she asks, dropping into the chair opposite and leaning forward, a mischievous curiosity in her eyes. "Sleeping well? Found anyone that can put up with you yet?"

"Look, Charlie, I'm tired, okay? I just want to get my proof that Eddie Redwood was a user, take it to my client, and get paid, alright?"

"See, now that's why we were never a good match," Charlie replies, a hint of sadness in her voice, despite the big smile on her face. "You're far too serious all the time."

I glare at her and bring my mug up to my mouth, downing another begrudging mouthful. Damn, it's good, though.

Charlie waits to see if I soften, and when I don't, she laughs quietly and shakes her head. "I'm afraid that I'm not going to be much help. When I heard what you were looking for, I pulled my records and had a look through them. No Eddie Redwoods at all."

"He could have used a false name," I grump. "Or had a proxy come and buy for him. Or bought a bit here and a bit from one of the other two."

Charlie rolls her eyes. "You know better than that. The people that buy from me don't buy from people like those two. They either stock up when I'm about or go to one of the other Elite Sellers. As for a false name or proxy, well…" She sighs. "I checked the reported levels that Eddie was carrying. I only made one sale for that much, and it definitely wasn't to Eddie Redwood. I seriously doubt that he was a proxy either."

"Who was it?"

Charlie pulls a small bundle of papers out from behind her cushion. She looks at them, and says, "I'm only giving you this because, despite anything else, I still look at you as a friend." She reaches across to me and adds, "The name's highlighted."

I put my mug down on the floor and take the papers. There, in the middle of the page, one name sticks out from behind bright neon-pink highlighter fluid. *Devin Carmichael.*

"Diu… *Fuck.*" I sigh.

Seven

I LEAVE CHARLIE with an awkward hug and a half-hearted promise to make time to visit sometime soon and catch up properly. We both know I won't keep that promise, but I say it every time anyway. We only dated for a year, but I fell harder and quicker than she did. There wasn't any specific trauma that caused it to end; we didn't fight, and neither of us cheated on the other, but for the last couple of months of the relationship, we slowly drifted apart anyway. We both saw what was happening, but neither of us did anything to try to stop it. *That* makes me bitter.

Unwanted trips down memory lane aside, though, she did at least give me what I needed, if not what I expected. Devin Carmichael being involved proves that the death wasn't an accident, so now I get to tell my client that she's not batshit crazy. Let's weigh that one up, shall we? On the positive side, my fee just doubled. Go me. On the downside, this just got a whole lot more complicated.

Open and shut, my ass, Hoove.

Eight

THE ADDRESS THAT Lori gave me was at the opposite end of the city, so I relented and took a cab. We're in that weird time now that comes after the end-of-work rush hour and before the burst of activity that comes when people start going for nights out. The upshot of that is the journey was quick, if a little overpriced. I'm just glad that the driver didn't notice Bert perching on top of his roof, or he'd have probably charged me more.

Lori lives in a small bungalow at the tail end of Forster Street, a small community of houses that appears to be an homage to the old world. Sure, the building materials are set by modern standards, but the style is derivative of anything but modern. Honestly, it wouldn't seem out of place if she had a white picket fence hidden away somewhere. The windows aren't on lockdown, and the older-style curtains hanging behind the metal sheeting are still open, but the lights are off. If she chose this area because of the vintage style, she could dislike the metal sheets the same as I do, albeit probably for reasons of taste rather than the convenience of spying on potential visitors.

Either that or she's fallen asleep before shutting up for the night. Given that she's in mourning, and that her car is still parked just outside the place, that's probably a good bet. If that's the case, though, she won't be asleep for much longer. I give the doorbell a couple of presses, and listen to the simple chime echo through the house. Just to be sure, I give the door a hard round of knocks too. I'd feel guilty, but she hired me to do a job, and to do that, I need to speak to her.

I spot a movement out of the corner of my eye, and turn to look at the house to the left of Lori's. The kitsch falls of fabric sway a little, and snap shut at a speed too precise to be the work of a breeze. Curtain twitcher. The one hobby that proves curiosity and paranoia never die. I guess that makes me—what? A blind twitcher?

Lori's neighbour's door clicks open and a homely looking elderly lady peeks her head around. "Excuse me, dear, were you looking for Miss Redwood?"

"Sorry to disturb you, ma'am," I reply, turning on my best saleswoman smile. "I was, yes. Is she not home this afternoon?"

"Afternoon? It's closer to evening now, love." She laughs. "I'm afraid not, though. Tonight's one of her meetings down at the Community Hall."

"Oh? Sorry, but could you point me towards it at all? I really need to speak with Miss Redwood, you see, but I don't really know the area too well. I tend to stick the Main Street area, and to be honest, I didn't know there was anywhere like this around here."

"Not many do, dear. We don't mind that, though. It keeps the place quite quiet. If you follow the road down that way," she says, pointing further down the road, "you'll see it soon enough. The sign's big enough that you shouldn't miss it."

I smile and nod gratefully. "Thank you, ma'am. And sorry again for the disturbance."

"Think nothing of it, dear," she says, and makes her way back inside.

I nod up to Bert, who has taken up residence on Lori's roof, and say quietly, "Stay." He shifts into a sitting position, mimicking the gargoyles of old that he was designed to resemble, and I start to make my way down towards the Community Hall, nodding politely to Lori's neighbour as she pulls her curtain back again to wave me on my way.

The road isn't long, but it does have one glaring eccentricity. The odd-numbered houses from one to twenty-seven go up one side, but there are no houses on the other. I have no idea whether the even numbers were at one point meant to exist or not, and I doubt that the residents do either. The road ends at a small traffic circle, with one road heading back the way I came, one heading off towards the northern city exit, and one heading back south towards my more familiar haunts.

At the opposite end of the circle, the road isn't long enough for me to call it an exit, but it does head into the car park of what looks like an old storage building. Were there not an oversized sign outside proclaiming the place as the Community Hall, I wouldn't have even considered that was what lay inside. The cold run-down exterior screams "abandoned warehouse," not "local social point," even with the handful of cars sitting idle outside.

Inside is a different story. Just beyond the double doors at the front is an unmanned main desk that could have been taken from any photo of the era when church halls were the centre of every community. There are no crucifixes or other religious iconography, though. God lost his grip on this place a long time ago, and the birth of intelligent AIs like Bert put the final nail in that coffin for a lot of people. He may not be the perfect imitation of life, but Bert and the others like him are close enough that the more arrogantly inclined of the species finally found their excuse to all but proclaim humans in the developmental industry as godlike. Now, instead of looking to the Bible for guidance, people just flick to the troubleshooting guide in their collection of digital manuals.

Figuring out where to go is easy. Hell, I wouldn't be much of a PI if I couldn't guess where the meeting was being held; there's only one corridor, to the right of the desk, and there's a lot of noise coming from behind the double doors at the end of said corridor. I wander down and shove the doors open without a second thought.

"Huh." I don't know what I was expecting to find inside, but it certainly wasn't this. The hall is spacious, easily bigger than my apartment times four, and that's a damn good thing. Tearing around the room are a—what do I even call them? A pack? Yeah, let's go with that. A pack of Tech Shifters.

I count three cats skulking around the edges of the room and occasionally pouncing on any other Shifters that stray too close to them. When they come near each other, they just keep moving, walking warily, and turning their heads to watch their fellow feline as they pass, with their shiny segmented tails pointed haughtily in the air. Off to the side, two tigers are play-fighting with each other, taking it in turns to raise big metallic paws up to the other's shoulder and barrelling them over. Once their playmate has been floored, they lunge forward and let the grounded Shifter roll them off to the side so that they can start again. Meanwhile, something that looks like a springbok is bounding merrily across the hall, weaving in out of four steel dogs that are eagerly chasing and fighting over a regular tennis ball, with the victor darting proudly back with its prize and dropping it at the feet of the one other human in the room.

I walk over as the lady launches the ball across the hall, sending the dogs off in a frenetic cacophony of growls, yips, and wagging tails. She looks over to me with a smile, and nods in greeting. There's nothing too much that stands out about her; she's pretty much an atypical bottle-blonde girl next door. Either that or all the Tech Shifters running about make her look plainer than she is.

"Cassandra Tam," I say, drawing up close to her. She nods again but doesn't return the introduction. I nod out towards the room and ask, "I don't suppose Lori Redwood is out there somewhere?"

Plain Jane takes the tennis ball from another of the dogs and launches it off towards the back of the room again.

She tuts a few times and turns to me, smiling kindly. "You're new to this, aren't you?"

"Pretty much," I concede.

"We don't use real names here."

"Is that a fear of reprisal thing, or a shame thing?"

She sighs and shakes her head. "Neither, usually. The one you're looking for is Ink."

"I see. And which one would she be?"

"The one on the stage." She nods to the chairs at the back wall and adds, "The meeting'll be over soon. If you want to wait, I'm sure she'll be happy to speak to you then."

She may as well have just said, "We're done talking now, leave." I show her the same courtesy that she's shown me and give my thanks in the form of a curt nod, then take myself off to the chairs and drop myself down onto the uncomfortable plastic.

The stage at the back of the room is fairly small compared to most these days, and the spotlights are all off, leaving it shadowed and virtually hidden. I scan from left to right a few times, and finally spot Ink curled up towards the back. Most of the Shifters running around down here have retained the polished silver look of the materials that make their gear, but Lori seems to have opted for something a little different for her alter ego. The shine is still the same, though I wouldn't have noticed if I hadn't been looking, but the flexible metal is obsidian black, giving her a degree of camouflage in the shadows. Since she's not out running with the others, it's probably a safe bet that she's left the stage lights off on purpose so she could achieve just that effect. With the stuff she has going on, I guess she doesn't want to lose contact with people but isn't in the mood to interact.

A clock hidden away in the corner of the room chimes, and the room comes to a near standstill. One of the dogs, a small Alsatian-looking thing, picks up the tennis ball and trots calmly over to Plain Jane. I can't tell for sure, but I get the impression from the barely visible human build under the suit that the dog is male. He drops the ball at her feet and sits up, panting through his mask. She drops down, picks the ball up with one hand, pets him with the other, then pulls a leash out of her pocket. She carefully clips the leather strap to the dog's collar, and holds out one hand, palm up. The Alsatian lifts one paw, drops it into her hand, and waits. She says something to him quietly, and stands up, leading him from the hall.

Most of the Tech Shifters have already left, and the others are filing out quite calmly. From the half-muffled *snaps* and *cracks* out in the reception area, the owners of the cars out front are clearly reverting to their normal appearance. There are definitely more animals than cars here, though. *I wonder if any of them are carpooling?*

A quiet and admittedly natural-sounding *mew* draws my attention to one of the oversized house cats as it slinks across the room. It sidles over and brushes up against me, purring quietly.

"Er, hi," I say, my discomfort pouring out of the two words like a geyser and dragging an embarrassed blush with them.

The cat looks up at me with strangely familiar eyes. I can tell from the way that they're twinkling that the kitty's inner-human is smiling. Seemingly satisfied, it saunters away, tail flicking proudly as it nudges the door open and disappears into the reception area. I'd complain, but the behaviour is remarkably authentic for pretty much every cat that I've ever met. Every single one that I've come across has sought ways to wind me up, usually by playing games like "Hunt the grumpy PI's toes" and "block the path to the beer like a wizard blocks a Balrog." After a moment, I realise why I recognised the cat's eyes. *Tobias Martin. He was a cheeky sod during the case too.*

I push myself up to my feet and look over to the stage. Lori—no, Ink—sits studying me. From the shape of the mask, she's undoubtedly a panther. Not as bulky as a real one, perhaps, but a panther nonetheless.

Ink steps casually down from the stage and pads past me, walking straight out through the door. I start to follow but stop myself and listen instead. I have no idea what Tech Shifters wear underneath their suits. For all I know, the various drivers could have had backpacks of clothes stuffed behind the reception desk ready for their Shift. Or they might have stored them in the toilets, wherever they are. The last thing I want to do is unexpectedly walk in on my client in the nude.

Instead of the metallic *clunk* that I was expecting, I get the creak of the doors opening again. Ink sticks her head in and stares at me, waiting.

After a moment, I walk towards the door and she backs out, letting them swing shut again. I push through and follow her outside, where we find Plain Jane waiting patiently by the last remaining car. I note that the Alsatian is in the back seat, head resting on the front passenger seat.

Ink sits herself down next to me and stares at Plain Jane for a moment. Jane nods, walks over, and hands me a door key attached to a camera-shaped key chain. "For her place," she says, nodding down towards Ink. "She'll show you the way."

I take the key and run it around in my hands a couple of times. "Thanks," I say. "And hey, I'm sorry if I offended you earlier. With the shame thing."

She smiles and shakes her head. "We're a strange bunch, I'll give you that. Personally, I find online gaming provides plenty of escapism for me, but my husband gets too frustrated for that."

"Oh. Is...um..." I say, glancing towards the car.

Plain Jane laughs. "That's him." She pulls another set of keys from her pocket and says, "I'll lock up here. You two can get going if you like."

Ink pushes up to her feet and trots off towards the traffic circle, while Plain Jane walks silently back to the hall, key spinning merrily around her finger. I guess the group isn't big on good-byes. I catch up with Ink, and she heads up the path, keeping slightly in front of me to lead the way. She moves naturally, like she was an actual panther and not just Lori Redwood in a suit. Her arms, I notice, are exactly the right length to allow her to walk on all fours without having to hunch or kick her legs out behind her. I'm pretty sure she wasn't that disproportionate when she came to my office. Nor were her legs shaped like they had haunches. The suits must be built to lean as closely towards realism as possible.

Ink glances back to make sure that I'm still following, catches me watching, and gives me a kitty smile, showing off the razor-sharp teeth hidden in the mask. She bounds ahead a few steps, comes to a stop next to her car, and sits back on her haunches, her tail swishing from side to side. I catch up quickly and roll my eyes.

"I already knew which one was yours. I stopped by before I came and picked you up." I walk towards the front door and nod subtly in the direction of the still twitching curtain next door. "Your neighbour there pointed me to the hall."

I give the key a twist and the door clicks open. Before I can push it the whole way, Ink nudges me to the side and trots in, coming to a stop by an open door, halfway up a small hallway. She waits for me to come in and shut the door, then hops her front legs up onto the doorframe, stretching herself like a house cat that's just come home after a successful hunt. She moves one large paw around the edge of the opening and taps a light switch, instantly flooding the adjoining room in light, then drops down with a soft *thud* and pads inside. Not sure what else to do, I follow quietly, and make it to the doorway just as she starts to deactivate her Tech Shifter gear.

Ink, still standing on all fours, jolts her shoulders up once, twice, three times, and a loud *clunk* sounds as both arms slide away from the body. Lori slips her arms out of the metal frames, flexes her fingers, and reaches back to her thighs. She taps several times and another hidden fastening comes noisily undone, causing the back legs to release their hold and allowing her to wriggle forward, leaving the metallic haunches behind.

Now on her hands and knees, Lori hunkers down and lowers her head. A rapid-fire *click-click-click-click-click* sounds and the thin strips of metal around Lori's torso snap out to the side, raising up in the air so that the frame looks like a giant hundred-legged spider pouncing on a small mouse or rat. With a loud *thwip*, the strips retract in unison, and roll up into a neat tube. The tail drops motionless, and there's a series of quiet *pops*, starting at the base of the metal spine and moving quickly up Lori's back and over the top of her head.

Lori sits up, folding her legs under herself, and reaches up to her mask. She slides the front of Ink's face open, and gently starts to pull the mask away from her head, unclipping it from the plugs that form her Mohawk. Once her head is free, she gives a well-practised flick of her wrists, and the rest of the spine pulls away from her back plugs, letting her place the thick metallic strip flat on its side at her feet.

She stretches and lets out a content grunt. Under the Tech Shifter gear, she's been wearing a skintight black Lycra bodysuit with visible padding over various points. The strips of metal that create Ink obviously run close to the skin too, meaning that the padding is purely there to alter the aesthetics of the final form. Even with the modifications, the outfit leaves little to the imagination. I already knew she was shorter than me, but I can now see what was hidden beneath the loose jacket and jeans that she wore the last time that I saw her. She's not particularly muscular, which is a surprise given how heavy Ink looks to wear, but she doesn't have the same layer of untoned mass that I have either. Hell, her whole body's like that. She's healthy looking, with the tightness of someone who likes to keep in shape but doesn't feel the need to pile on the muscle mass. The real kick for me is that, with two glaring exceptions, she's sufficiently smaller than me to remind me that my future is probably to end up looking like a moustache-less miniature Captain Hoover.

I shake my head and start to study the connectors running along the bottom of the spinal strip, searching for something to say. I wouldn't normally pay this much attention to a client's body, but the combination of her leaving it on display like that and the memories that being around Charlie dug out of their tidy little grave in the back of my mind have reminded me how long I've been hanging out in my apartment with just Bert and my film collection for company.

Finally, I manage, "So the connectors go all the way down?"

Lori looks at me, a playful glint creeping into her eyes. She laughs, and stretches her arms up behind her head, then twists away from me so that I can see from the back of her head, all the way down to the base of her spine. *A little more and I'd get to see just below that too*, I think, and as if she's read my mind, Lori gives a smooth extra twist. I could swear she gave her ass a little shake too. Struggling to get my mind out of the gutter and back on to my poorly improvised question, I force my attention to the way that the bodysuit has rubber-flanked holes designed to grip around the outside of her body plugs.

"Yup," she says, twisting back to face me. "All the way down the back anyway. It's funny, though, most people start with asking why I do it. We must have really shaken you, huh?"

"Shaken. That's one way to put it," I grunt and lean against the doorway. Searching awkwardly for a way to keep the conversation moving, I dig deep and manage, "I was surprised that there weren't any hybrids at the hall."

"Nah, it's more the Furs that go for the hybrids. There are exceptions, I'm sure, but not in our group. That said, we do borrow from them with this stuff. The way they used to build quad-suits formed the basis for the arm extensions on the Tech Shifter gear. If we didn't do that, we'd still be on our hands and knees and wearing kneepads like some of the traditionalists."

"Traditionalists, huh? So if you're not a Fur, then that makes you...?"

"Afraid so," she replies, dropping into a cross-legged position. "Card-carrying Second F. Can't say I care for the term, though. 'Fetishist' never did feel right. Not for Ink anyway."

I shrug. "Hey, I'm not judging."

"It wouldn't bother me if you were. I do what I do because I want to do it. If it's within the realms of the law and people still have an issue with it, then that's their problem more than mine. I don't like the term because people hear 'fetish' and automatically think it's sexual. Sure, that's part of it for some, but the majority of Pet-Players don't do it for that."

"Pet-Players," I repeat, tilting my head curiously. "If it's not sexual, then why do you do it?"

Lori smiles widely. "See? I knew you'd get there eventually. It's escapism. A way to get away from everything that bogs us down during the week."

I step into the room and find a two-seater couch pressed tightly against the wall next to the door. I sit down and nod at the spinal connectors. "Seems like a lot of trouble to go to just to unwind."

"It's not unwinding, it's running. At least for me." Lori shrugs and gets to her feet. "If it works, it works," she says and walks towards another door at the opposite end of the room. She flicks the light on, steps in, then I hear the sound of running water splashing in the bottom of a kettle. "So, what was that you were saying to Jane? About offence and shame, I mean?"

So her name really is Jane. Go figure. "I was apologising. While the meeting was still going on, she told me that no one uses their real names there, and I asked if it was 'cause of a fear of reprisal or shame about what they're doing."

Lori steps back into the room and leans against the door, her arms crossed. She raises an eyebrow at me, and says, "I thought you said you weren't judging."

I sigh and shake my head, dropping my gaze to my feet. "I wasn't trying to. I just made an assumption that was way off the mark." I look up apologetically, and Lori drops her hands behind her back.

"Don't worry about it. We've all heard worse than that. Still, in a way, you're lucky that you had a chance to offend *anyone*. No one would have spoken to you while they're shifted, and I doubt the drivers would have that soon after a shift either. Jane doesn't always have the time to come along, and most of the groups are Strays, so you could have just found yourself in there alone with the wildlife. I'm assuming she pointed out which one I was?"

"Yeah. And 'Strays'?"

"Jane is happy to indulge Murphy, that's the Alsatian, in his interests. So, in terms of the gathering, they're Master and Pet. That's why he gets a collar and the rest of us don't. We don't have Masters, so we're Strays. I mean, most of them have partners outside the meetings, but none of them really like to join in."

"So most of *them* have partners. What about you?" I ask, and immediately feel my own jaw drop in shock at the vaguely seductive tone that had crept into my voice.

Lori stares at me for a moment, then laughs and walks back into what I'm assuming is the kitchen without answering the question.

I wait until she's disappeared behind the door and face-palm myself. "Damn you, Charlie," I groan.

Lori rematerializes a moment later, and hands me a hot mug. "Coffee," she says. "Or there's beer in the fridge if you prefer. I'm guessing that you didn't come here just to show off your ignorance about Tech Shifting, so I'm going to go and get washed and changed. When I'm back, we can talk."

I nod, eager to kick this mood and try to get back on course. "Good. So, are you gonna leave, uhm...Ink...on the floor, or did you want me to put it away somewhere for you?"

Lori's eyes light up and she says, "I normally put *her* away before I get changed, but I'm loving how flustered she's making you, so I'm gonna leave her out a little longer. I'll pack her up before we talk, but for now, she can be your punishment for asking a client inappropriate questions." And with that, she slides from the room and up to the end of the hall.

Nine

LORI WASHES QUICKLY and returns to the living room, prolonging the awkwardness that I have around what I've come to think of as Ink's shell long enough to take my mug and refill the kettle. The body-hugging Lycra is gone, and she's now wearing a pair of loose-fitting tracksuit bottoms and a plain T-shirt that reveals the hint of tattoos on both her upper arms. Apparently satisfied at last that she's punished me enough, she slings Ink's spinal piece over her shoulder and hoists the leg sections under her arms, then trots out of the room. She returns empty-handed, and by the time she's made the next round of drinks, I'm feeling a little more like myself.

"So what brings you this far out?" Lori asks, unable to keep the hopeful tone out of her voice.

I clasp my fingers together and decide to just be honest about what's been going on. "When I took this case on, I made it clear that I believed the most likely outcome would be that the police were correct and that Eddie simply OD'd on synth stimulants. To that end, I've spent most of today talking to the local dealers who have been active over the last month. My thinking was that, given your belief that he didn't use the stuff, if I could prove that Eddie bought the stimulants, then that should be enough to prove the scenario to you."

Lori takes a deep breath and holds it, waiting for me to continue. There's a tension in her eyes now, and she's biting her bottom lip, the action making her look far less hardened than her normal appearance would have you believe. Never judge a book by its cover? In most cases, I don't agree with that. In my line of work, if it looks like a thug, it probably is a thug. With Lori, though, the side of her that she's shown tonight is enough to make a believer out of me, at least in her case.

"The officially released reports confirm that Eddie's body contained traces of Flash7, an upgraded version of one of the all-time bestselling stimulants on the market. Based on their findings, they figure he'd taken a little over three hundred milligrams of the stuff. Assuming that none of the dealers were lying to me, which in all honesty, I doubt they were, only one person bought that high a quantity of Flash7, and it wasn't your brother. I initially considered the possibility that if Eddie was keeping his habit a secret then he could have used a proxy, but now that I have a name, I can all but guarantee that wasn't the case. The man who killed your brother is named Devin Carmichael, of that I'm certain."

For a moment, Lori simply stares at me, tears glistening under the ceiling lights. She lets out a short, uncomfortable laugh, and rubs a shaking hand across her eyes. "Then...do we tell the police, or do we need more evidence first?"

I shake my head. "If they'd wanted to, the PD could have figured this much out. When it comes to VJ Addicts, though, if it looks like an overdose, then as far as they're concerned, it *is* an overdose. If they'd done some digging and come up with the same name, they would have still called it the exact same way."

"I don't understand," Lori replies, screwing her face up in confusion.

"That's where the Police Department is a big old bag of contradictions. See, the lower ranks are mostly good people. While the upper echelons are notoriously corrupt, the small fry do their jobs, following the letter of the law. The problem is, the law itself is broken, and it's dictated by the self-same corrupt bosses that prevent them from being all that they could be. What that means is that, sometimes, bad people get away with things for no other reason than someone at the top wants them to. The knock-on effect of that is that the law allows some other bad people to sneak their way out of their due punishment too.

"When that happens, the guys who just want to make the world a safer place for honest citizens, have to make a choice. They can let a couple of criminals slide on by, or they can act within the twisted rules that they're forced to obey. Nine times out of ten, they can't bring themselves to be what their bosses want them to become, and they turn a blind eye. Every now and then, though, someone just bad enough to get the good cops frustrated finds themselves walking scot-free.

"When someone's the wrong type of dirty, Devin Carmichael is the cleaner. See, a good cop can do a bad thing and still convince themselves that they're the same person they were before the act. If it gets the scum off the street, even if it means putting them in a hole, then they can take solace in that."

"Wait," Lori cut in. "Are you saying that the police wouldn't touch this Devin Carmichael guy because *they* hire him to *kill* people?"

"It's not just the police, but that's about the size of it, yeah."

"I...I can't believe that. I mean, I know that they aren't...but assassins?" She shakes her head. "I just can't."

"Whether you believe it or not makes no difference. It's still the truth."

Lori grips her tracksuit bottoms tightly and bows her head. Her tears fall freely, soaking into the lightweight material as she asks, "So where does that leave me? Am I supposed to just accept that Eddie was murdered and move on?"

Yes. That's what I want to say. *Yes* is easier, for me and for her. But I can't do that because seeing her in tears like this reminds me of how I was back in Vancouver. I know how much I lost because I couldn't just accept the way the world is. I know how many sleepless nights I've had since, the memories of one night haunting so many others. But I also know that, no matter how much I lost, I'd do it all again in a heartbeat because it was the right thing to do.

"Not necessarily," I say, and Lori looks up, surprise on her waterlogged face. "Devin Carmichael does not kill off his own back. If he killed your brother, then someone paid him to do it."

"But you said that if they see his name, then the police still won't do anything about it."

I nod. "I know one who *may*, but only if we can give him something to prove who hired Devin and why."

Lori wipes her tears and takes a deep breath. "So what do I need to do?" she asks.

"For now, just think. The report that you made for me focused mainly on the crime scene and what little he'd told you about trying to go Pro. What I need is for you to think about what your brother was like, who he hung out with, and whether he could have made any enemies. On top of that, I want you to think about whether anyone out there would have a reason to hurt *you*. Most likely, this is all about Eddie, but I don't want to discount the possibility that he was a victim in a whole different vendetta."

Lori's face tells me she hadn't considered that as a possibility. It also tells me that I just scared the life out of her. Her mind's probably racing right about now, running through every little moment of paranoia that she's ever had, trying to fill in the gaps and link it back to her brother's murder. Finally, she sighs, pushes up to her feet, and walks over to a small bookshelf tucked away opposite the door to the kitchen.

She comes back with a large ring binder, and hands it to me. "My work portfolio. When I'm Ink, *that's* what I'm running from."

I flip the hardback front open and find a photo mounted on a thin sheet of card. The picture is a wide shot from a protest a couple of years back. The protesters were simply marching for higher pay, and someone made an anonymous call to the police, shouting and screaming about violence in the streets. The then-captain didn't bother checking and sent a squad out with orders to subdue the "rioters" by any means necessary. The resulting bloodshed cost the captain his job, and let Hoover step in. The violence was a tragedy, but I can't say I'm upset about the outcome. From the way that the police are piling forward in the shot, Lori must have caught things just as the trouble kicked off and the second wave started trying to confiscate cameras.

The next page is a photo of the artificial lake situated just outside the city. The synthetic greenery is smeared with a thick black substance that's spilled into the water and entrapped what looks like a small bird. The oil, or whatever it is, is covered in pieces of litter, so it's probably fair to assume that at least one person saw it and thought they may as well use it as a bin rather than call someone to clean it up. Hey, if it's wrecked already, who'd care, right?

Next is a shot that I recognise; the sorrowful visage of the elderly father of a local woman who had been falsely accused of murdering a child. She'd been arrested during a time when people were getting restless with the lack of positive action that the police seemed to take in relation to violent crimes, and so her guilt was presumed confirmed from the get-go. She was given fifteen years and was killed two days into her sentence. I know the case well because, less than one month after her murder, I proved her innocence beyond a doubt and helped win her a retroactive pardon. Her father was grateful, even more so when I told him that I'd waive my fee. What he really wanted was his daughter back, and that was something I just couldn't give him. As far as I was concerned, he'd suffered enough already and didn't need my jumped-up fees to add to his woes.

Flicking through the folder, I see it's full of photos like that; all capturing a side of the city that's existed from day one but that the brochures promising a fresh start and a happy life in New Hopeland never show you.

"You can't help them," Lori sighs. "Not straightaway. The photo has to come first, because that's your job. The people suffering…It's too late for most of them anyway. You know, every now and then you come across things that are just *the* perfect shot for an article that you know isn't lined up, but *needs* to be written. And you know that you've got to snap what's happening before you can even try to do anything else, because if you don't, the article won't ever exist, and telling people is all you really *can* do." She shakes her head sadly and continues, "Most of the time, all we manage to do is to get people talking about an issue for a day or two. After that, they move on to whatever's the next big talking point that it's cool to get involved in. Sometimes, though, we do make a difference."

Lori flips a few pages over and stops on one large shot of a homeless person. The man is bloody, bruised, and lying unconscious outside the local government buildings. Less than five feet away, the former Local Housing Officer, I can never remember his name, stands talking to the press, ignoring the man on the ground.

"The Local Housing Officer seat was never one that was up for election, but when the role opened up, Jed Wilson campaigned like it was. He went out and spoke to the citizens, made promises, kissed babies, all of it. By acting like a presidential candidate, he got enough people excited that the local officials had no choice but to give him the job."

"He lasted two years, didn't he?" I ask.

Lori nods. "Yeah. At the start, he seemed to be making good on his promises with housing development and shelters, but those of us out rooting around on slow news weeks started seeing things that weren't what they seemed. Everything he did, he did on the cheap. That wouldn't matter if he had major constraints on funding, but he was getting a lot of money coming in from both the public funds and the charitable donations the locals were making. On top of that, every success story that he threw in front of the press was always *too* good. These were down-and-out people that he was helping, sure, but they were clean. No major problems, no dark past, just plenty of sob stories and happily ever afters. We *all* thought that something was going on."

"So the guy in the photo wasn't one of his successes, I take it?"

"No. And there were countless others like him. I got lucky with that one, though. I was on my way to take some shots of Jed's press conference when I found the guy. Seeing him that close by without the LHO batting an eyelid was too good a chance to miss. I snapped the shot, grabbed an interviewer that I knew was just waiting for a chance to take Jed down, and we took the poor guy off to the hospital. He'd been beaten by Jed's security team when he went to try to plead for a place in one of the shelters."

"Overcrowding?" I try.

"That's what they told him. In truth, though? They weren't even close to overcrowded. This guy, Bob Sherwood, just wasn't the sort of person that they wanted about when the TV cameras were due to stop by. He was still an alcoholic, still wanted for multiple counts of breaking and entering, and he absolutely stank. Jed preferred the newly homeless with their down-on-their-luck tales of redundancy and marital splits. That photo and the accompanying interview kick-started a series of investigations that showed Jed had been taking around 85 percent of all funding for himself. He lost his job, his credibility, and his freedom. If Eddie was killed as a way to get back at me, it'd have to be something to do with my work. This photo is the only one that I've ever taken that's had a long-lasting effect on anything."

Taking down crooked politicians, eh? I push back the gamut of painful memories and muster my best reassuring smile. "What you're thinking makes sense. You'll be happy to know, though, that there's no way Jed Wilson could have hired Devin Carmichael."

"Why not?"

"'Cause Devin may be a killer, but he has a moral code. There are certain types of people that he won't work for, and crooked politicians happen to be among them. Now me, I'm a great believer in the theory that all politicians are crooked, whereas Devin believes in the old "innocent until proven guilty" shtick. Jed Wilson got jail time, so there's no chance he'd take him on."

"So you're telling me he'd work for a crooked cop, but not a crooked politician?"

I shrug. "He used to say that if he worked for a crooked cop, then he was still broadly working in the public's interest, but if he worked for a crooked politician, then he was only working in *their* best interest."

Lori's shoulders sag, and she lets out a relieved sigh. She takes the folder back from me and shuts the cover, then walks back to the bookshelf. "You seem to know a lot about him," she says. "Devin Carmichael, I mean."

I nod. "I work alongside the corrupt and the scum. You meet a lot of interesting people that way. Believe it or not, Devin's one of the nicer ones you could come across. Unless he's been hired to take care of you, of course."

Lori laughs bitterly. "He killed my brother. I don't think that nice is a word I can apply to him."

"Fair enough," I reply. "And if we're being honest here, we don't know one hundred percent that he killed Eddie yet. All we have is a set of numbers that make it likely. I'm gonna tackle that, though."

"How?"

"I'm gonna ask him. He won't tell me who hired him, but if I slap a warrant on him for information, he'll tell me whether he did it or not. Until then, I'm working on the basis that he did, which brings me back to needing you to think things through. When you first came to me, you said that you thought someone in the company that was going to hire Eddie could have killed him. Did you have any reason in particular to think that?"

"No," Lori replies sadly, shaking her head. "No, you were right. I was just reaching. It was the only thing that came to mind."

"Well, given Devin's usual fees, an executive in a high-powered company isn't a bad bet. You're sure that you don't know which company it was that he was in contact with?" Loris shakes her head again. "There are ways to find out. I'm going to use one of the Governmental Monitoring Offices to try to discover if he had any lengthy virtual meetings with anyone working for someone of that level, and maybe check who else he saw regularly there too. I'd rather not go into that blind if I can help it, though, so I'm gonna need a favour."

"Anything," Lori replies, her voice resolute.

"Can you get me into your brother's house? I want to see the place where he died."

Lori flinches, but says, "Sure. I can do that."

"Good. I noticed that the official photo the reports were using was one of yours. I know this is hard, but if you took any other photos of the place, I want you to bring them with you. I'm guessing the place has been cleaned, but if possible, I want to see what was about at the time that he died. Maybe that will give us some clues."

"I have a couple. I'll get them loaded up on my tablet," she says, and stands up again.

"You don't have to do it now. Look, Lori, thinking that your brother was murdered and having someone tell you that you're probably right are two very different things. This can all wait until the morning. I never knew your brother, so I won't know if anything was out of place. You will. For that, I'm gonna need you rested and alert. For now, the best thing that you can do is get some sleep."

Lori starts to protest, but a yawn cuts her words off. Funny how the mention of sleep can do that to you, especially if you really are tired and trying to hide it. "Okay," she says at last. "Can we start early, though?"

"Sure," I reply, getting to my feet. "Eight good for you?"

"Yeah. Yeah, eight is fine."

"Good," I say, and make my way towards the front door. Lori follows behind me, her shoulders slumping under a mix of exhaustion and nervousness. "If you think of anything else, any names or even just some crazy random thoughts about either of you, write them down, but try not to dwell on them. We can sort through anything that you come up with tomorrow."

Lori nods, and I open the door. "Hey," she says. "You don't drive, right? Did you need a ride back?"

I smile but shake my head. "You rest. I'll get a cab."

"Okay," she says, and her face drops.

I step out into the night and let the cool air hit me. She's hurting, I get that, but I can at least try to make her smile before I go. "Hey," I say, turning back towards her. "When I come to get you tomorrow, I'm not gonna have to take you for walkies, am I?"

Lori looks at me and blinks. A small giggle rises in her throat, and she replies, "Only if you want to. Good night, Cassie."

"Good night, Lori," I smile, then turn and walk away. Fifteen seconds later, the door clicks shut, and I finally manage to drop the mild flirtatious glint from my eyes. "Damn you, Charlie."

"Caw," Bert comments, gliding down to perch on my shoulder.

Ten

IT TAKES ME half an hour to make it to the apartment block in South Main Street. I've had enough of walking, so I take the elevator all the way up and head to the only door on the top floor. I give it five hard raps with my knuckles, and listen. When I hear the slow *tromp* of boots heading towards the other side, I place one hand against the outer doorframe and lift my phone up with the other, the screen already illuminated.

The door swings inward, and a man steps into the light. He's tall, a little over six foot, and built with what most would call a chiselled physique. Even if I didn't already know that, it would be abundantly obvious now, as he seems to have decided that it's the right weather to go topless. At least he's wearing his jeans and boots, I guess.

The man tilts his cowboy hat back and peers down at the warrant on my phone screen. He smiles. "Well, someone's all business tonight," he says, his voice dripping with a slow Southern drawl.

"Devin," I reply, "I'm tired, and I'm in no mood to fuck around, Okay?"

Devin Carmichael laughs and runs his hand over the stubble littering his square jaw. "That's fine with me, darlin'. If ya went to the trouble of getting a warrant all set up, ya must be pretty desperate."

"Eddie Redwood, Virtual Junkie Addict, died last week with the remains of over three hundred milligrams of Flash7 in him. Did you kill him?"

"Now, if you've come all the way over here to be asking me that, I reckon ya already know the answer." I glare, and he rolls his eyes. "Yeah, I killed him. What about it?"

"Who hired you?" Even though he's confirmed my suspicions, I can't believe he gave up the information quite so easily.

Devin crosses his arms and leans casually against the other side of the doorframe, forcing the door all the way back. "Warrants don't get ya that much, Caz."

I sigh and drop my phone arm. "Can't blame a gal for trying. All right, let me ask you one more question. If I said that I had no idea who hired you, but name your price and I'll hire you to go kill them right now, what would you say?"

"I'd say no can do, darlin'," he replies, smiling wide enough for his overly white teeth to catch the light from the hallway.

"Fine," I say, and walk away without another word. The door clicks shut almost instantly.

I knew that he wouldn't tell me who hired him. That he wouldn't just turn around and kill the client for the right price means he's not changed either. Devin likes a good story. He likes to know not only who's hiring him, but why they want someone dead. There's not a single person out there that's too high up or too important for him to take down if his client has the right reasons, but if he feels that something's up, he won't take the job. Knowing he's still the same old killer means that I've got a better chance of hunting his client down myself. If he'd started taking cases indiscriminately, then that would open up the possibility of Eddie's death just being a random execution, bought with no grudges or reasoning other than "I've got the money, and I can." That sort of thing is hard to prove unless they get careless.

I make it out into the night, check the time on my phone, and give a sharp whistle. Bert comes swooping down from a windowsill somewhere further up the apartment block, and lands gently on my shoulder.

I tickle him under his chin again. "Let's get some sleep," I say, and hit the speed dial for a cab.

Eleven

I CLOSE MY eyes in my bed and open them again in Charlie's living room. The dream is the same one that I have every time I visit her. I am unseen, as solid as the barest whisper of a ghost, and I can neither touch nor change the scenes that play out in front of me. All I can do is watch and wait it out.

I push myself away from the wall, the sound of Charlie and me laughing about some stupid joke from the TV following me as I walk the room. The screen is blank, but I still remember the joke. It was the story of a teenage party told by a heavily accented Scotsman, and the footage was a little blurred due to its age. Charlie preferred the comedians of the twenty-first century to the modern crop with their anecdotes of misspent virtual sessions. She told me once that the older comedians' experiences felt more real to her, and that the reality for most modern humans was too far removed from reality for her taste.

The memory fades, and another slides seamlessly into its place: The two of us, dancing closely to music from a set of house speakers as silent as the TV was blank. The song was an instrumental ballad by a local jazz act that we'd seen earlier in the evening. I try to hum a few bars, but like always, my voice is silent, even to me.

I walk from the room and into the hallway, making my way towards the kitchen while my memories continue their slowly turning trip around the back of the couch. If I stay, they'll fade out and leave behind the time that I managed to spill two cups of coffee down myself after I slipped on one of Charlie's shoes, left ridiculously in the middle of the floor, then jump to me hiding in her arms as the monsters on screen close in on the heroine.

Every part of the history trip leads to the same point; those last few hours when we spoke properly for the last time. I can't escape any of it, 'cause we took in the whole house with those moments. It was like we both knew exactly what was happening and we wanted to leave one last mark in every room before we said good-bye.

I stop in the doorway at the end of the hall, watching the two of us cooking a spaghetti bolognaise on the hob next to the counter that we'd leaned on when we shared our first kiss. We were drunk and rougher than we were in the days that followed, but that was okay. The two of us met during a case, and we kept in touch. Six meetings later, we'd both resolved to tell the other how we felt, and opted for alcoholic assistance to guide us on the way. As a result, I came to her place barely able to stand, and she met me at the door, barely able to walk in a straight line.

If I stay here long enough, Charlie will go to the fridge and grab two beers. She'll turn, look at me in the doorway, and I'll see it in her eyes. Back in the living room, we'll talk, and the last bit of fight will fall away from both of us. Out here in the hallway, we'll go to the door and I'll hold her tight, but let go when she sags and grips my jacket. I'll turn then and leave in silence. If the dream ever took me outside, I'd make it halfway down her drive and collapse onto all fours. I'd bury my head against the concrete, grip my hair and cry, then sit up, wipe my eyes, and walk away, a little more closed than I used to be. Right now, up in the bathroom, we'll cross in the doorway, and share another short kiss. The warmth will be gone from it.

Instead, I walk up the stairs, ignore the sound of us trying to figure out how to unclog the toilet, and head to the bedroom. I sit down on the windowsill just as the final memory of the night fades in.

The last night that we spent together.

She teases me, while I wait for the memory of her touch to come rushing back, but just like my voice, I won't find it here. I won't feel the warmth of her breath on my neck, the sharp bite of her nails on my back, or the softness of her lips on my body. I won't smell the flowery scent of her hair, and my head won't pound with the desperate longing to try to make the night last forever.

All I can do is watch and listen as she finally lets me take over, her hand and voice guiding me to her favourite spots. The end comes quickly for both of us then, and we collapse onto the bed, our sweaty bodies clinging tightly to each other as we silently drift into an uneasy sleep.

Just like my memory self, I wearily close my eyes and...

Twelve

THE SOUND OF the alarm hits me like a freight train, jolting me upright. I double over in bed, struggling to catch my breath. My hair is plastered to my forehead, and judging by the sting shooting through my eyes, I've been crying too.

"Some hard-ass you are," I grumble, using my thumb and index finger to wipe my face and push the mass of tangles back behind my ears. I should have known that this would happen. Every damn time I see Charlie, all it takes is for something familiar to click in my head, and I get *this*. It wouldn't matter, but everything about her is familiar. The crease by her eyes when she grins. The playful lilt to her voice when she calls my name. The way her top sways over her hips when she walks. The rhythmic sound of her footsteps. Her hair, her scent, her damn coffee. I know all of it like I know the back of my hand.

Everything that I remember about being with Charlie is good. I should be able to smile about that, but I can't. I don't get to have little things bring back happy moments of reminiscing, and I don't get to be grateful for what I had. So what did one year of happiness buy me? Bad dreams and a need to push people away if they get too close. Oh, and the fact that I feel like I have to deke out on someone I actually like so that I *don't* get this crap.

"Diu," I growl, slamming my sweat-covered fist into the mattress. "Diu! Diu! Diu!"

A light metallic *clank* makes its way across the office part of the main room, and Bert comes to a stop in my bedroom doorway. "Caw?" he asks.

The first time that he did that, I was bewildered. Over time, I've come to get used to him checking in on me. It's the two sides of his programming interacting with each other. The combat part knew that there was no threat, and the pet part knew that it should try to comfort me. Over time, and a lot of these little episodes, I've gotten used to his squat frame appearing once I wake up.

"I'm fine, Bert," I say. "Go make sure that you're charged. It could be a long one today."

"Caw," he replies, giving a little bow, then turns and waddles his way back out again.

I wait until he's disappeared around the doorframe, and mumble to myself, "Metal claws they came a-clacking, clacking at my chamber door. Quoth the Bert."

"Caw, caw," he replies from somewhere near the kitchen.

I shake my head and smile to myself. "Silly little bugger."

Thirteen

I MAKE MY way to the Industrial Park just behind Main Street first, heading straight for the Local Government's Virtual Monitoring Office. It's early, but that place runs twenty-four-seven, the same as most virtual-based business, so I can guarantee that someone will be there.

I go inside and find that the guy at the main desk is someone whose name I can never remember but who always seems to remember mine. He's the sort of person that, if I insisted on following my father's footsteps in that regard, my grandfather would have settled for me marrying, despite not being from the "old world". Why would he be fine? Because he's atypically ordinary, has a nice demeanour, a good job, and, above all else, is male.

Most of my family moved with the times, in some cases even adapting their religious beliefs to fit with the world around them, but Granddad, bless him, liked tradition. What that meant was that my one high school girlfriend was, to him at least, a "study buddy". The few who came after that? Close friends, nothing more. I took that as a positive. Most people tell me I'm weird when I say that, but the fact is, I've known a lot of people who were completely ostracised by their family when they came out. Granddad loved me enough to not want to do that, so he chose to ignore that part of me rather than let it cause him to walk away from me. Would I have preferred acceptance? Sure I would have. But I had that from my parents, and I'd rather have denial than conflict.

Mr. X is as helpful as he always is, at least once I finish completing one of the warrants stored on the PD's online system for my use. Deciding what information I'm going to need is difficult, though. I won't be carrying out the work myself, that wouldn't be allowed, no matter who I was, but I don't want to leave myself with too much to go through afterward. If the need to clear my head wasn't as dire as it is, I would have headed to Lori first and based my searches on whatever I turned up at her brother's house. As it is, there's no way that I'd be effective, so this guy gets the joy of my cheery disposition first.

In the end, I settle for three things. First, a full tracking of Eddie's final log-in to the virtual world. That should show where he went, who he spoke to, and who else was in the vicinity that may have seen or heard something. If he died calling out the culprit's name, for example, that would be a stunning, but strangely not unheard of, piece of luck. Second, I asked for a list of IP and MAC addresses used by Eddie over the last month before his death, including the real-world addresses that they related to. Finally, I requested the details of anyone that Eddie met multiple times over the same period and spent more than ten minutes with at a time, including names, IP and MAC addresses, and the relevant real-world addresses for each. It's a broader search than I'd like, but it does mean that, if nothing turns up at his house, then I may still get lucky with Eddie's online history.

I finish filling in my request, leave it with Mr. X, and go to call yet another cab.

Fourteen

I MAKE IT to Lori's place a little after 07:55, and find that she's already dressed and ready to go. She's opted for a slightly different ensemble this time, with a lightweight long-sleeved burgundy sweater hanging over a pair of black baggy trousers and heavy-looking well-worn boots. The whole outfit would be classed as "scruff" by the local fashion-focused types; the slight stretch in the jumper, the small tears at the bottom of the trousers, and the scraped-away front of the boots, revealing the shine of steel toecaps, all add to the depreciation in style value. To me, it's all just suitably casual. If she's comfortable, then she's going to be able to pick up more than if she's feeling uneasy.

We stand in silence for a moment, me on her porch, watching her watch me from just inside her house. Lori is the first to make any significant move, leaning herself against the open door and crossing one arm just below her breasts, so that she can rest the elbow of the other on top of her hand and make a show of gently squeezing her lips between her thumb and index finger. Her pale blue eyes, icy in the shadow of the day's black eyeliner and matching eye shadow, move slowly up and down as she studies me.

"Hmm," she says.

"What?" I reply, mentally kicking myself for the irritability in my tone.

"I was just wondering if you only had one set of clothes, or just loads of the same thing."

I look down at myself, noting my usual polished shoes, plain black trousers, and white work shirt from the men's section. The tie is different than yesterday. Yesterday, it was a black tiger embossed on a black background, while today it's a black dragon on a black background. I like the subtlety of it, but I guess it's not overly apparent unless you get a closer look.

"Loads of the same," I say at last, my academy training on communication kicking in as a method of self-defence and causing me to parrot her wording. "And I only wear them for work. It's like a uniform or a character. Helps me separate one bit of my life from the other."

"Cool," she replies with a nod. She's probably drawing parallels between what I've said and how she views Ink. To be fair, if that's the case, she's not a million miles off. She starts to gather her things, and asks, "So, what sort of stuff do you wear when you're not working?"

I wait for her to start shutting the door, then turn my back to her and say, "Remember when you came visiting?" The creaking of the door comes to an abrupt stop. I let the silence hang for a moment. Then, smiling smugly, I look back over my shoulder and give Lori a wink. A little voice in the back of my head says, *blushing looks good on her*, but I ignore it in case Charlie creeps in again.

Lori blinks, laughs, and pulls the door closed.

Fifteen

WE ARRIVE AT Eddie's house on Cornick Crescent less than half an hour later. The ride over started off fairly jovial. We mostly joked about people we drove by and talked about stupid things that we'd done when working. The closer that we got to the house, though, the edgier Lori became. She spent the final stretch of the journey staring silently into traffic while she tapped nervously on the steering wheel. Now that we're here, she's retreating into herself; jamming her hands into her pockets and standing stiffly as we survey the room where her brother died.

For all the assumptions that I made at the start of the case, Eddie kept a far nicer home than Mark Farlow and the Hollands. While their place was a pretty typical Nest, nothing here even hints at an Addict being the sole resident. The log-in chair and gear in the living room are in good condition and look like they belong in a small-to-mid-level business premises rather than someone's home. Shelves line one wall, packed full of neatly ordered books on a variety of subjects, ranging from music and philosophy to cooking and programming. One small glass table sits a little way off from the chair, clean bar the normal layer of dust that things tend to gather over a week or so. Even compared to the rest of the road, number seventeen is a nice place.

Every room in the house is like that: almost obsessively ordered and kitted out in a retro-modern style with the feel of someone getting by far better than I am. "So what was he doing for a living to be able to afford a place like this? Freelance tech work or something like that?"

"No," Lori replies. "I think that was part of his problem. We both had a decent inheritance from our grandparents. That would have been about seven or eight years ago, I think. I already had my job and just kept on working, but he was still struggling to find someone to take him on. He spent big initially, then just budgeted well and got by on the money while he was job hunting. The longer you're unemployed, though, the tougher it is to get something."

"True enough. Can I see the pictures that you took?"

Lori nods and taps her tablet screen a few times. After a moment, she passes it across with three photos tiled across the screen. "Those were the only ones that I saved."

The top left photo is the one from the news sites. Rendered in black and white, it's fairly artsy for what it is. The shot shows Eddie's arm hanging over the side of the log-in chair, dangling limp and lifeless. On the underside of Eddie's forearm, a tattoo is partially visible. I can make out some lettering, but there isn't enough to read.

"Any idea what the tattoo on his forearm said?" I ask.

"It was a quote," Lori replies. "I think it was from a poem. *A poor life this, if full of care*, or something like that?"

"*We have no time to stand and stare*," I finish.

"That's right. He got it just before he started getting heavily into virtual work."

I nod and enlarge the second photo on the screen. This one is a full-body shot of Eddie in the chair. He still has the needle that killed him in the hand that wasn't visible in the last photo. Devin would have likely made use of Eddie's semi-comatose state to make sure that it was his own hand that pumped the shit into his veins, so that's not surprising. If Devin left his own fingerprints on it, Hoover would have told me from the get-go. Eddie's headset looks like a pretty recent model, but that fits with the rest of his gear. His clothing is understated; just a pair of comfortable jogging bottoms and a T-shirt with some sort of logo on. I'd question it, but I've seen it before in the window of one of the local mainstream stores. It's not a licensed product; it's just a pattern that they plastered on this year's run of discounted designs.

The third and final photo is taken from an angle to the side of Eddie's head. The closeness to his head has resulted in a slight blurring of the headset and sagging lower jaw. Hanging just below this, the hand holding the needle is in better focus. There's probably a market for stuff like this. If she wanted to, Lori could declare it a visual comment on the millions of faceless sufferers of addiction and substance abuse that you pass every day without ever knowing it, and the critics would eat it up in an effort to seem edgy. If it weren't for the circumstances, I'd be tempted to suggest it to Lori as a way to make a quick buck.

What makes the third photo useful is that it also shows the near edge of a small glass table in the background, displaying the bottom of a heavy-looking book. Zooming in shows the open page as number eighty-four, and the visible part of the bottom line reads, "...popularised by Clement Burch during the dawn of the modern..."

I wave Lori over and show her the close-up section. "Do you know what would have happened to the book?"

"I tidied up after the police were done. It'll be back on the shelf."

"Okay. Do you remember which one it was?"

Lori shakes her head. "No, sorry. Is it important?"

"I don't know. It could give us an idea of what he was doing on the day that he died. That may point us to who, if anyone, he was meeting with, which might give us a lead on someone who saw him that day. Or he may have just been reading for the hell of it, or trying to fix something of his own. Without looking, though, we won't know for sure."

Lori stares at the screen for a moment. Her brow wrinkles, and she looks over her shoulder at the crowded bookshelves. "It looks like a pretty big one. Less than half his books are even near that size. We have the page number and the last line, so..."

My phone buzzes, and a generic ringtone blares out from the handset. It's an annoying little jingle, but it gets my attention far quicker than anything I could customise the phone with. As far as I'm concerned, using a favourite track just risks you either getting sick of the song or ignoring the call so that you can listen. Having something that you struggle to bear makes you more likely to pick up quickly.

I pull the handset out of my pocket, look at the screen, and sigh. "See if you can find the book," I say to Lori. "I'll take this outside."

Lori nods, but her expression is full of suspicion. She's right to be suspicious. I've been waiting for this call since last night; I just didn't think that it would come this soon. I tap the little green Accept button on the screen and stroll calmly from the room and towards the front door.

"Hey," I say.

Captain Hoover's voice comes through the handset speakers, his moustache audibly bristling against his own phone. "You want to tell me why I've just had Inspector Bergesson on the phone telling me that we let you question Devin Carmichael?"

"Probably 'cause I questioned Devin Carmichael last night," I state, my voice neutral.

"Funny, Caz. Real funny."

"You know what I'm working on."

"Yeah, I do. That's what confuses me about this. I told you that it was an open-and-shut case. Sad as any sob story, but for most people, it's just another Addict that checked himself outta the hotel without meaning to."

"Devin admitted to killing him."

"Shit," Hoover sighs, drawing the word out. "And you're still working the case?"

"Yep."

"You know what Devin being involved means, Caz. What exactly do you think that you're gonna get outta this?"

"Ten thousand," I say, smiling to myself. "That, and I'm gonna prove who hired Devin to take Eddie Redwood down and personally dump all the evidence on your desk."

Hoover groans and asks, "And then what? Huh?"

"What do you mean, 'and then what'? C'mon, Hoove, you know how it works. I give you the evidence, and you make the arrest. You're about the only guy there that I know would act on it, even with Devin's involvement."

"And what if I told you that I'd been ordered to leave this case well enough alone?"

My breath catches, and a sudden chill runs down my back. "Seriously?"

"Real fucking seriously, like on my badge seriously. You know me, Caz. I'd love to help you out here, but I can't."

I narrow my eyes. Hoover swearing is never a good sign. It means that he's been shit on from a great height, and he ain't happy about it. "You wanna tell me why?"

"You ever heard of a single damn case where Devin's killed someone and the client got as far as the court? Me neither. The higher-ups reckon that if we take *one* that way, then we've got to open them *all* up. That wouldn't just mean giving the bad guys a tough time, that would mean sending half my staff down with them."

I slump back against the wall and lift a weary hand up to my head, pushing my hair back. "Diu."

"Pretty much sums it up," he replies. When I don't say anything in response, he asks, "So what're you gonna do?"

I glance over towards the window that should lead into the room I left Lori in and close my eyes. "Keep working the case. My client's pretty cut up. Maybe proving who hired Devin...maybe that'll be enough to give her some closure."

"I hope so," Hoover says, and I can hear the sincerity in his voice.

"For what it's worth, I used the second warrant at the Monitoring Office. Am I still good for the third?"

"Technically no, 'cause you haven't filed it yet. If it happens to come across my desk, though...it's easy to miss something small like a date, right? But don't go thinking that we'll be able to give you a fourth on this one."

"Thanks, Hoove."

"Don't mention it. Just try to get it all wrapped up ASAP."

He hangs up before I can reply. With most people, I take that as pretty rude, but I've learned over time that Andrew Hoover isn't one for good-byes. I slip my phone back into my pocket and head back to the living room, bringing myself to a stop in the doorway. Lori is bent over the glass table, skimming through the pages of an open book and, when she hears me coming, looks up in silence, her expression asking if the call was about the case.

"I went to visit Devin Carmichael last night," I say. "He confirmed that he was hired to kill Eddie."

Lori nods, but her expression remains unchanged. She's smart enough to realise that something else is going on here.

"I would have told you sooner, but I didn't want it to affect you while we were here. The thing is, the PD just had an earful from the higher-ups about me questioning him. You remember when I said that the higher up you go, the more corrupt they get? Well, Captain Hoover is about as high as you can go and still know that you're dealing with a good cop. He's not untouchable, though."

"Was that who was on the phone?"

"Yeah."

"They're not going to do anything, even if we prove who killed him, are they?"

"No."

"So what happens now?"

"That's up to you. You *could* decide to leave things as they stand. You'll know that you were right, and I'll waive the rest of my fee 'cause I didn't finish the case."

"And if I say that I want to carry on anyway?"

Something in her tone says that she's already made up her mind. There's a resolute edge there, almost making it a challenge. She may as well have just said, "Don't think for one moment that you're walking away from this one just yet, Cassie."

I smile. "Then we'll find out who hired Devin Carmichael to kill your brother."

"Good," she says, and taps the pages of the book that she's opened up on the table. "I found the book." I walk over to stand beside her and she continues, "It's a manual for a couple of linked virtual systems; SnapDragon Suite, Light Break, and NSX."

"NSX...Nine Seconds Transfer?"

"That's the one. My bank uses it, and it's quicker than its name makes out."

"Okay, but what are SnapDragon and Light Break?"

Lori flicks to the front of the book and runs her finger down the index list. "Looks like SnapDragon is a data capture suite and Light Break..." She shakes her head, and flips a couple of pages. Any book where the index runs into the double figures is way too long for me. Finally, she says, "I think it's some sort of security software. It looks like most of the book is about how the three systems interact and what problems they can cause for each other."

"So what was the page that Eddie was reading?"

Lori flicks back to the first page of the index again and says, "Uhm...historical problems with the SnapDragon Suite that occasionally turn up in newer versions."

I walk over to the bookshelves and skim through the titles. "Looks like he has one more book on SnapDragon, one on Light Break, and one—no, two more on NSX. I don't suppose he used any non-Virtual machines?"

"Not that I know of. Even knowing he didn't buy the...Flash7?" she says, looking at me to make the name of the drug a question. I nod and she says, "Even then, he was still a Virtual Junkie. As far as I know, he did all his computer work in the virtual environment."

"The newer headsets are all locked by retinal scans, so we won't be able to just log into his account and see what he was up to. If he'd had a tablet or something like that, we could have unlocked it."

"Couldn't we get his headset unlocked too? There must be people who can do that. I mean, you hear about them having problems all the time and locking users out."

"Manufacturers and the original seller offer unlock services, but they'll only unlock someone else's gear for two reasons. The first is if the police require it for an investigation. If Hoover hadn't already been given his orders, I could have tried to get him to sign off on it, but there's no way that he'll do it now."

"What's the second reason that they'd do it?"

"If they're wiping it for resale."

"Ah."

"Yeah. There are other ways to figure out what he was doing, or at least who he was meeting with. Do you know the Industrial Park near Main Street?"

"Of course."

"Good. I asked the Monitoring Office to do some research on Eddie's last month online for me. They should be done by now, so if you're up for taking a trip, our best bet is probably to head there, then back to my office."

Lori gently shuts the book, the weight of the hardback cover making a quiet *thud* despite her controlled movement, and places it carefully back in its spot on the shelf.

"Let's go," she says, and walks purposefully out towards the front door.

Sixteen

THE DOORS TO the Virtual Monitoring Office slide open, and Mr. X looks up from his desk. With me walking in front, he spots me first and gives me his usual pleasant smile. Once Lori steps out from behind me, his mood seems to stick, but his face changes completely. His eyes light up, and his eyebrows arch into a relaxed curve. The corners of his mouth drop down a little and move out to the side, letting his mouth open wider and fall into a smile that I wouldn't have known was more natural than the one I normally see if I hadn't seen it grow out from the other. I guess what *I* was getting was professional courtesy. Good to know.

"Oh," Mr. X says, not even trying to hide his surprise. "Hi, Lori."

"Hi, Jer," Lori replies. "How are the kids?"

"Same as ever; messy, funny, and full of opinions that they're too young to have." His face becomes serious then, and his voice takes on a quieter, almost soothing tone. "And what about you? How are *you* holding up?"

Lori shrugs. "Better, I guess. It's a long road, you know?"

Jer, which I'm guessing is short for Jeremy, nods. "Well, if there's anything that I or Nicole can do to help, let us know. The spare room's still available if you want to get away from it all for a while, and you know how much the kids love Ink."

Lori smiles. It's not the full-faced playful smile that she's been giving me, but rather a quiet smile, full of gratitude and familiarity. "Thank you," she replies. "I'll be fine, though. If you've been helping Cassie figure out what happened to Eddie, then you're helping me plenty."

Jeremy relaxes back into his chair a little, and taps his chin a few times with his index and middle finger. "Is that right? You know, I didn't even check the names you put on the request forms. I wonder..." He lets his gaze drift to the ceiling for a moment, then drops it back to me and gets to his feet, drumming his hands on the desk in front of him. "You know how to fill in the receipt forms, right?"

I nod.

"Good," he says, placing his tablet on the desk and swiping through the screens. "If you could start going through those, I'll be back in a minute."

Jeremy trots off towards the main office without waiting for a response, leaving me to sigh and start signing and dating on the relevant lines. I make a lot of requests from this place, so I pretty much know where to jump to on instinct now, and with no policy changes having taken place recently, I don't need to bother reading through the terms and conditions either. In the same way, I know exactly how much they're gonna charge me for both the printed summary and the USB stick containing the full version of the requested data.

"So Ink's kid-friendly then?" I ask without looking up from the screen.

"Sure," Lori replies. "She looks all tough and scary, but she's just a big house cat, really."

"Only without the arrogant strutting or the 'I meant to do that' attitude when she does something wrong, right?"

"Oh, I've done all that before," Lori giggles. "If you're playing a character, you've got to play it well."

I glance up at her and realise that she is both completely serious and not in the least bit embarrassed by the fact. "All the world's a stage," I say. "And one woman in her time plays many parts."

"Yup. It's just that some of us play more than one part at once." She grins.

I finish signing the payment details page just as Jeremy makes his return to the desk. He pulls a brown envelope out of a drawer. The name "Miss C Tam" is scrawled along the front in blue marker pen. From the envelope, he takes a small USB memory stick, and places it on the desk. Next, he grabs a blue marker pen from the pot next to him and draws a large dot at the tip of the stick. Finally, he takes another memory stick from his pocket, places it in the envelope, and drops the memory stick from the desk into his pocket in its place.

I raise a curious eyebrow at Jeremy, and he says, "We had a bit of an issue with staff accidentally giving out the wrong memory sticks to customers, so we started marking our copies with blue dots. See, your copy contains the data requested, and nothing else. Our copy has the requested data in one folder, and some other folders with all sorts of linked data, such as brief profiles of relevant people, their most common log-in points, and so on."

"So which one did you just put in the envelope?"

"Well, they've both got blue dots now, so who knows? If you happen to have accidentally ended up with the unedited office copy, though, I'm sure that you'd return the stick to us at your earliest convenience, wouldn't you?"

"You're not going to get in trouble for this, are you?" Lori asks, a tinge of concern in her voice.

"Of course not. The audits run monthly, and ours was yesterday, so as long as the stick gets back to me before this time next month, I'll be able to drop it back into filing and no one will be any the wiser."

"It'll be back before then," I assure him. "If I copy anything useful, will that show up in the audit?"

"Not a chance," Jeremy says. "It'll show up if you edit anything, though, so don't make any changes to the documents on the stick."

"Okay," I say, taking the envelope. I stop myself as I'm leaving and turn to Jeremy again. "Sorry, but why are you doing this?"

Jeremy smiles at me, his genuine smile this time, and replies, "Because Lori Redwood has helped my family more than she'd ever admit. You just make sure that you use that to get her whatever she needs to get through this."

I nod, but don't return the smile. Hey, if we're playing roles today, I'm sticking with professional and hard-ass. Lori, on the other hand, not only returns his smile but leans across the desk, and gives him a tight hug. "Thanks, Jer," she whispers.

Jeremy pats her back and whispers back, "Don't mention it."

And with that, we make our way out of the building, a little heavier on data than I expected to be. I wait until we're almost at Lori's car before I glance at her and say, "You must have done something pretty major to help Jeremy and his family if he's willing to give us all this in return."

Lori hops in front of me and rests herself against the door to the driver's seat. "Nuh-uh," she replies, giving me that playful smile again and waggling one raised finger. "That's *his* business. You'll get nothing out of me, copper."

I roll my eyes and say, "Fair enough," then walk around to the passenger side.

Seventeen

THE DOOR TO my office creaks if you move it too slowly. I could fix it easily enough, but I choose not to. The reason for that goes all the way back to my high school days, when all the other girls were scared of me. See, the popular girls all liked to *talk*, especially if it was behind someone's back. They knew that what they said would get back to the target eventually, and a lot of the time, they set it up to make sure that happened. If harsh words didn't cut someone down, the ringleaders were confident that they could take their target in a fight. That was part of how they picked their victims; focus on the weak and only go for the stronger ones when they're already down.

Case in point, Stacy Woods. She was the self-proclaimed queen of the school, and in her mind, she was the toughest bitch to walk the planet. Even without her *muscle*, and by that I mean two tall girls with big mouths, she intimidated those around her with sheer attitude and the promise of scratching your eyes out with her ridiculously long false nails. I was the daughter of a cop. To call what they did fighting seemed ridiculous to me. It was bullying, pure and simple, and it was cowardly beyond belief. The school knew what was going on but didn't seem to be doing anything about it, at least in the eyes of those of us out in the battlefield that was our teenage lives. So, I took matters into my own hands.

I spent some time making myself look like the sort of person that Stacy would go for. I was already taller than most, a little chunky, and of a mixed heritage, so she had plenty to pick on. Throw in some carefully planned bouts of emotion, and I soon became her new plaything. Her words washed over me, but I turned on the tears whenever I knew that she was in earshot. Finally, after a solid month of this, I *snapped* and challenged her to a fight.

Stacy turned up expecting hair-pulling, slapping, and screeching like a fox in mating season. She got a right hook, a broken nose, and a kick that bruised two ribs. Stacy was never the same after that, and the other would-be queens started to back off after her fall. On the downside, the rest of the girls in school became scared of me. Even some of my friends started to distance themselves for fear that they'd upset me. No amount of explaining my plan could fix that. But that was okay. I stopped the worst of the bullying for the duration of my time there, saving a lot of girls a lot of hassle that they never knew would have come their way.

My parents, of course, got called into the school for a talk. While they were there, they admonished me in the way that they were meant to, but when we got home, they asked me what had really happened. I explained everything. While they didn't approve of my methods, they did understand why I did it. That was when my mother gave me a single piece of advice that's stuck with me ever since. "Stacy thought that she was the biggest, baddest dog in the yard," she said. "Then she came across you and learned that there was someone out there who was bigger and badder than she could ever be. There will always be someone tougher than you, Caz, always. Don't ever forget that, and don't let yourself think that you're invincible."

Maybe I'm just being paranoid, but in my line of work, I tend to find that people dislike me. And there are a lot of bigger, badder, and tougher dogs than me in this city. If they decide to deal with me, it won't be in a fistfight on a school field. They also won't rush in, all guns blazing. They'll take it slow and try not to draw attention to themselves. Probably. If they do that, and the creak of the door doesn't draw *my* attention, it will at least mask the quiet little *clack-clack* of steel talons on the hardwood floor as my clever little security system gets himself into position.

With the early part of the day being set aside for information gathering, I figured that it would be safe to leave Bert at home. Not wanting to have him mistake Lori for an intruder, I shove the door to the apartment open at speed and make sure that I enter first. Lori shuts the door and steps up beside me just as my shiny little guard dog trundles out of the bedroom. He fixes her with his glowing red eyes, tilts his head to the side, and says, "Caw."

"Lori, Bert. Bert, Lori," I say, then point a stern finger at Bert and add, "Be nice."

"Caw," he says, then wanders into the kitchen and starts to scale the counter.

"Is that a Familiar?" Lori asks.

"He," I correct. "And yeah. He was in for maintenance when you dropped by the first time, or he'd have met you at the door."

"He's adorable. Like a little metal gargoyle."

"I thought so too," I reply, smiling to myself. "He's a cocky little bugger, though, especially if he thinks he's got you scared."

"Aww, how could anyone be scared of him?"

"He's primarily a Protector Class unit, so he can do some real damage if he needs to." I turn to Bert and ask, "You like to break stuff, don't cha, Bert?"

"Caw, caw."

I put my hands on my hips in mock anger and say, "Well, that's just rude." Lori giggles, and I turn to look at her. "What?"

"Oh, nothing."

"No, come on. What?"

"It's just...you get all freaked out around Ink, but with Bert, you're like, so comfortable that you're like a completely different person. I was just thinking that there's hope for you yet."

I roll my eyes. "Well, it's good to know that I'm not a completely hopeless case." I flick the kettle on, then walk over to the table and pull both the printed summary and the memory stick out of the envelope. We avoided going over the details of the printed sheet during the car journey, just in case anything clicked and the shock drew Lori's attention enough to make us crash. As a result, the car journey took half the length of time that it should have. Even after her complete disregard for road safety, I did let Lori have a quick skim read in the elevator on the way up to my floor, though. Eddie had had multiple meetings with two people during his last month alive, all of which ranged in length from half an hour to three hours. I wake my tablet from sleep mode and slot the memory stick into the least troublesome of the three USB ports. This one likes to cut out every now and then. The other two like to work every now and then. "You're sure that you don't recognise either name?"

"No. I mean, there's *something* familiar about Dean Hollister's name, but I don't know what it is. And I don't know Carl Sanders at all." She pauses, then adds, "It sucks that Eddie didn't meet anyone on the day that he..."

"Actually, that's pretty useful to know."

"How so?" she asks, a hint of hopefulness welling up in her voice.

"It adds fuel to the fire. If anyone tries to shoot the Devin angle down, we can point out some useful facts to combat it. First up, people who use synths tend to inject themselves immediately before or immediately after logging in. Second, when people *do* accidentally OD, it takes a good hour for the effects to happen, by which time the initial buzz has worn off and the victim has started going about their normal routines. With the amount of Flash7 that Eddie appears to have had in his body..." I say, then spot Lori wince. I smile sympathetically and say, "Sorry. But with those levels, it would have been quicker. Add in that you said he didn't use at all, and we can safely say that the half hour he was online was how long it took. People don't just log on to do nothing if they're using; they want to feel everything. That he didn't leave the log-in room and there were no initial danger signs on the scans means that he wasn't looking for a cheap thrill. If it really was an accidental OD, he should have been wandering around, and someone should have seen him. Those are facts that can't be covered up with the usual media spin that the PD spokespeople use."

Finally catching up, the tablet cuts in. "Good...afternoon, Cassandra. How may I be of assistance?"

"Copy external media device contents to server six. Primary folder, open case files. Subfolder, Redwood Lori." The screen flashes up the rotating circle of impenetrably slow processing, and I shake my head. "Sorry. This may take a while."

"No problem," Lori replies. "Is it age, or is it just gunked up with bloatware?"

"Probably both," I concede. We sit in an awkward silence then, watching the circle complete slow rotation after slow rotation. Finally, I ask, "So hey, out of interest, what made you come to me with your brother's case?"

Relief lifts Lori's delicate lips into a gentle smile. I'm glad I wasn't the only one feeling awkward. "You were recommended to me by a friend."

"Tobias Martin, right?"

"That's right," she replies, and leans back into her chair, crossing her arms. The smile remains on her face, letting me know that she's not upset, and her eyes light up with curiosity. "Okay, Detective, spill. How did you know that I was talking about Tobias?"

"When you came to me with the case, I sort of remembered your name. I thought it was Eddie's that I recognised, but when I searched my case files, it was yours that I found."

"Is that right?" She laughs. "And what do your files say about me?"

"Just that Tobias mentioned you when I was interviewing him. I wanted to check for potential suspects for his case, and your name came up." Lori raises an eyebrow at me, and I shake a hand to wave down any suspicions. "Don't worry. He was only saying that you wouldn't have been the one who...uhm..."

"Stole his money," she finishes for me. "It's okay. I know about what happened."

I nod and breathe a sigh of relief. "The reason I brought it up, is that he said something I was curious about." I look to Lori to see if it's okay to continue, or if she's uncomfortable talking about something a friend had said. She tilts her head and beckons me to continue with her hand, so I say, "He told me that you were his Alpha. Or *our* Alpha. Thinking about it, he definitely said 'our', so I'm guessing that he meant the social group?"

Lori bursts out laughing, and my jaw drops open in surprise. "You look absolutely terrified," she says. "Honestly, Cassie, you don't have to be nervous about asking questions about Tech Shifting. That you're asking rather than making assumptions or buying into stereotypes is actually quite refreshing."

I lean back into my chair, mimicking the cross-armed pose that Lori had held before she collapsed into fits of laughter. Try as I might, I can only muster a half-hearted glare to go with it.

"Well, I'm glad I amuse you so much," I grunt.

"Oh, you really do. We should hang out more after this is all done. I could have some great fun with you."

I feel a blush rise up in my cheeks, but I'm too slow to do anything about it, and Lori laughs again. Unable to think of a suitable response, I just drop my head to the table in frustration. Lori reaches over and rubs my shoulder playfully, and I feel goose bumps rise under my shirt. I didn't get that reaction when I hugged Charlie yesterday. But then, I kept myself in "work mode" with Charlie. *Has it really been two years since I let myself relax around someone?*

"It's cool," Lori says, cutting my thoughts short. "This is good for me. I need something to distract me from what's going on."

"Oh?" I say, peering up from my hunched-over position. "So I'm just a distraction to you, then. Well, now I'm heartbroken."

Lori wags an accusatory finger. "Come on, you know I didn't mean it like that," she says, and I smile to myself at the mild panic that she's trying and, most importantly, failing to keep out of her voice. "And heartbroken? Laying it on a bit thick there, aren't you?"

I cross my arms under my chin, and give Lori my best puppy dog eyes and pout. "I'll have you know that I'm a very emotional person. Couldn't you tell?"

We stare at each other in silence, frozen in place, until, finally, we both break at once and start laughing again. "Alpha, Alpha," I say. "Tell me about this whole Alpha thing before I begin to feel any more awkward."

"Honestly?" Lori replies, struggling to compose herself. "I have no idea. I guess it's because I sort of run the meetings. I book the hall, collect any money towards the costs, and just, you know, deal with any issues. I guess I do mediate if there are any clashes, but that really just involves jumping in and growling a lot, making them back off, that sort of thing. I didn't know that Tobias viewed me as an Alpha, though. I wonder if the others do."

"You could ask them."

"Nah, I think that I've filled my awkwardness quota for the month." Lori gives an exaggerated seated bow. "I shall just have to accept my rule gracefully and get on with it."

"Files transfer complete," the tablet says, cutting off any reply that I could have given. I slide the memory stick out of the port and start checking that the files are functioning correctly.

The kettle clicks off, and Lori asks, "Did you want me to...?"

"Yeah, if you don't mind," I reply, opening the requested information document from its new home in my personal file store. "Tea and coffee are in the cupboard above the kettle, milk's in the fridge. Mine's a coffee, strong. Help yourself to whatever you want."

"Do you have any sugar?"

"I did, but someone threw it all over the floor."

Lori glances at Bert, and he stares back at her, lowering the strength of his eye lights to make it look like he's glaring. She shakes her head and looks back at me. "So why'd he do that?"

"The sugar *attacked* me."

"Oh, right...wait, what?"

I look at her and give a gentle smile. "It fell out of the cupboard and landed on my head. Bert, deciding that it was clearly some sort of miniature paper-packaged assassin, went for it and nullified the threat." I shrug. "To be honest, I think he knew full well that it was just a bag of sugar. I hadn't taken him out for a while, so he was probably just bored."

"Huh. I didn't know that Familiars got bored."

"Not all of them do," I say, turning back to the tablet. "Protector Classes don't at all, but Bert has a bit of Family Class programming in him too. I insisted on that. The last thing I wanted was a living weapon wandering around my apartment destroying everything. Now, when he does something like that, I can put it down to him being doglike or catlike."

"Catlike?" Lori repeats, her voice dripping with mock offence. "I'll have you know that Ink is far better behaved."

"Of course she is. That's why your doorframe was covered in claw marks."

Lori shrugs. "A kitty has to keep her claws trimmed."

"She needs to work on her memory too."

"What do you mean?" Lori replies, sitting back in the chair opposite me. She slides a cup of coffee across to me, and I take a mouthful. It's not bad, actually. A little lower on milk than I'd like, but I can handle that.

"According to the brief profile in the additional stuff that Jeremy gave us, Dean Hollister is the founder and CEO of six large companies. I've done a quick web search and two of them are pretty interesting. The first is Hollister and Holtz, a joint venture with Dieter Holtz. That one's primarily responsible for bringing software from both men's other companies together into one grouping. The software in question was Holtz's NSX and Hollister's SnapDragon Suite and Light Break."

"Ah. So what's the other interesting one?"

"Shift Source Limited."

"Really? He runs SSL?"

"Yeah. It says here that he was one of the original pioneers of the Tech Shifting concept. Apparently, he designed the prototype systems that allow the plugs and the suits to work together, as well as making a couple of physical adjustments to the general design of the suits themselves. So, chances are you either spotted his name in one of Eddie's books, or you remembered it from when you bought Ink. Maybe both. Given the books we found in his house, and the fact that the locations of his meetings with Hollister are all virtual world offices, I'd guess that Eddie was trying to get a job with Hollister and Holtz."

"Would the CEO be present for job interviews, though?"

I cross my arms behind my head and stretch my shoulders out. "Not usually, no, but who knows? Hollister's a hugely successful multimillionaire. Maybe he's picky about who he hires and likes to take a hands-on approach to recruitment. The job could have been something high up that fell under Hollister's direct management, or have been part of a project that he had a particular interest in. There could be any number of reasons for him to take an interest in Eddie. But the files say that he met Hollister seven times over the course of the month, which seems a bit high to me. Again, there may well be a reasonable explanation, but we won't know for sure unless we talk to him."

"I suppose," Lori replies, nervousness creeping into her voice. "Didn't you say that the guy who was contracted to kill him is expensive too?"

"Devin Carmichael, and yes. Hollister definitely has the means to pay him; we just don't know if he has a motive."

"Okay. So what about Carl Sanders?"

I swipe across to the file on Sanders and read silently through the first couple of lines. "Does the name Gary Locke mean anything to you?"

"Gary Locke," she repeats, drawing the words out. Her eyes narrow, and she clicks her tongue. "Is there a photo of him?"

I nod and spin the tablet around. The picture on the screen is of a man who looks like he's in his early thirties, but with a vaguely fashionable flop to his mid-length hair. He has a determined look in his eyes, and his designer stubble-covered jaw is set in a relaxed smirk. Lori leans over the table to get a better look, and my own gaze drifts up to do the same.

I barely have time to register my disappointment that she doesn't seem to wear low-cut tops like Charlie does before she nods, sits back down, and says, "Gaz. Gaz Locke. He was one of Eddie's friends. I think they met in…uhm…college, maybe? What does he have to do with Carl Sanders, though?"

"He was born Carl Sanders but changed his name to Gary Locke four and a half years ago," I reply, rotating the tablet back towards me and skimming further down the file while I talk. "It looks like he kept his old name for business stuff. Eddie had the same number of meetings with him as he did with Hollister. Do you know if they kept in touch outside the virtual world?"

"A little, yeah. I definitely met Gaz once or twice while I was visiting, but..." She trails off.

"Eddie was a Virtual Junkie and spent more time online than he did offline, right?"

Lori nods.

"When you met him on those occasions, what was Gaz like?"

"I don't know, really. It was usually a sort of 'hi, bye' thing with him."

"Okay. Is he likely to be friendly if we turn up on his doorstep?"

"No idea."

"In that case..." I say, turning to look over my shoulder. "Hey, Bert! Looks like we're going out. You want to tag along?"

"Caw."

Eighteen

GARY LOCKE, AS it happens, lives only two blocks away from me, in Morton Heights. Like most people these days, he lives in an apartment. The reason for this is that the city was built with the idea of housing large swathes of people in an economical manner, and making it easier for the incoming businesses to encourage their staff to live locally. While you wouldn't think it to look at her wardrobe, the fact that Lori is living in a bungalow actually places her pretty high on the financial ladder. Whether rented or owned, it'll no doubt be worth a lot more than my own modest living-quarters-cum-business-area. Throw in her lack of complaint about my fee and the fact that Tech Shifting suits are far from cheap, and you've got a pretty good indicator that she's living comfortably. Whether that's through work, the inheritance that she and Eddie got from their grandparents, or a combination of both remains to be seen.

Not that it matters. My point is, that judging by the condition of the building that we're standing outside of, Gary is not exactly a high earner. If anything, I wouldn't be surprised if there were a couple of Nests on the block. Given that he hung out with Eddie, who was a self-confessed VJ Addict, it could even be that he runs one.

I send Bert up to the third-floor level with orders to track us and intervene if he either hears my signal or reads that something is wrong. Here's hoping Gary Locke doesn't start brandishing the sugar.

Lori and I make our way into the building and head straight for the elevators. We ignore the security guard at the main desk, and he returns the gesture in kind, keeping his head buried squarely in the dull light of his phone screen. The elevator shudders and jolts its way up the three flights, but gets us there in one piece. Gary's apartment is at the back of the block, meaning that Bert will be scaling his way around the outside of the building right about now, looking for a potential entrance if it's needed. For us, though, the direct approach is fine.

I knock on the door and take a step back, stopping so that I'm to the side of Lori, but still central to the door opening. If he recognises Lori, that may result in us getting a warmer welcome, so I don't want to hide her from view. At the same time, questioning Gary is *my* job, so I want to make my role the focal point when he answers the door. When nothing happens, I knock again and resume my position.

Just as the silence kicks my internal paranoia engine into overdrive and the idea of a serial murderer of VJ Addicts on the loose jumps up as an idea, a heavy-footed shuffling echoes out from behind the door. And so we wait. The sound of three old-style, non-electronic locks clicking open precedes the slow creak of the door being pulled back, opening inward.

The man in front of us looks a little worse for wear compared to the photo on Jeremy's files. His eyes are a bit sunken, and the sweat dripping off the ends of his hair is weighing it down, causing it to cling to his face just below his ears. His clothes have a light odour to them that reminds me of out-of-date plums. The reason for the *scrape-thud* sound of his steps is also now clear; his left knee is supported by a hefty-sized brace like the ones you see on professional athletes when they're recovering from an injury, and he's carrying a crutch under his left arm. Looking at the slight sag in his build, it wouldn't be hard to think that he might have once been a sportsman of some sort, but he certainly isn't now.

"Cassandra Tam, PI," I say, and offer my hand. "Gary Locke, I assume?"

He looks at me warily, then turns his head towards Lori. There's a flash of something in his eyes, but it fades quickly and is replaced by a frown.

"Hi, Gaz," she tries. "It's me, Lori. Lori Redwood. We met a couple of times at Eddie's."

The man nods solemnly and takes my hand. "I pr-prefer Gaz," he says, and shuffles himself to the side. He nods down the small hallway and licks his dry-looking lips. "Please, come in."

Upon entering, I note that one of the hallway doors is wide open, leading to a surprisingly tidy bedroom. The other door is shut and probably leads to the bathroom. At the end of the hall, the room opens out into an open-plan space with the kitchen on the right and a living room to the left. A decent-looking log-in chair sits snugly against the back wall of the living room, facing out towards the kitchen. Two chairs are pushed up against the opposite wall that separates the living room and the probably-bathroom.

The door to my own apartment opens straight into the three-part kitchen, office, and living room area, the bedroom and bathroom sit at the far end, both behind closed doors with no hallway to separate them. While the larger size and the layout put it at a higher end of the market than places like this or the Holland-Farlow Nest, it does annoy me slightly that I'm essentially living in a similar state as the Junkies. I shouldn't judge. Really. There are some nice Addicts out there—I met a fair few of them when I stayed at Charlie's—but it does grate on me. I've always thought that I should be better than them. I mean, I haven't fallen into the trappings of addiction or anything like that, so to see any similarity between us is a knock. Or maybe it's just that being around them reminds me of *her*.

"Sorry," Gaz says, following in behind us. He makes his way across the room and slumps into the log-in chair. "I was online. The system told me that someone was at the door, but with my leg, it takes me a while to get up."

"Don't worry about it," I say. "We turned up unannounced, so it's not like you had time to prepare for us."

"Thank you," he says and turns towards Lori. "And, how are y-you, Lori? I was sad to hear about Eddie."

"I'm okay," Lori replies, then moves a laptop from the seat of one of the chairs and sits down. "It was Eddie that we wanted to talk to you about, actually."

"Oh?" he says, making the sound a question, then lurches forward and starts up a coughing fit. He slaps his own chest a few times and sits back again. "I'm sure that you know I'm an Addict," he wheezes. "Unfortunately, I could never afford the healthcare that Eddie could, so I'll have to ask you to forgive me if I struggle a little."

"That's no problem," I say, sitting in the chair next to Lori, and turning on my most pleasant false smile. "Still, that looks like a nice chair. What do you do for a living?"

"Right now, I am between jobs," he sighs. "The chair was a gift. Eddie was generous like that. M-Miss Tam, was it?" I nod, and he continues, "You introduced yourself as a PI. May I ask what brings you here today?"

I look to Lori and ask, "Did you want to explain that?"

Lori nods and lets out a deep sigh. She looks up at Gaz and says, "I was the one who found Eddie."

"I see. That must have been hard for you."

"Hard. That's an understatement. Seeing him slumped there, lifeless, the needle still in his hand..." She shakes her head and looks down at her knees, her hands tightening on her baggy trousers, bunching the material in her grip. "The police said that he died of an accidental overdose of Flash7, but I could never believe that. Eddie was just so against stimulant use, you know? He used to tell me how he was keeping his experience pure so that it didn't affect him if he went for a job with a Pro company. He was desperate to move from Addict to Pro. It just didn't make sense for him to do it."

Lori pauses, and I give her a chance to continue. When she doesn't, I take over. "Lori hired me to look into Eddie's death for her. We've spent the last few days running through everything that we can think of in case this wasn't an accidental overdose, as the police said."

"Ah, I see. And have you found anything suspicious?"

"Not yet," I lie, and lean forward, dropping my elbows onto my thighs and my chin into my hands. On the way over here, I briefed Lori not to let Gaz know that we had any evidence at all. If he was involved in any way, telling him that we think this was a murder would only spook him and make him close up. At the same time, a flat "no" would make the visit seem pointless and raise suspicions, *if* he was involved. A simple "not yet" shows intent, but it isn't strong enough to cause a shutdown. A slip-up, maybe, but not a complete shutdown. "As much I am bound to follow my client's wishes," I continue, "I do have to consider the possibility that Eddie *was* a user, and simply kept his stimulant habit a secret. I understand that you and he were close friends, and so I was hoping that you may be able to confirm whether this was the case."

Gaz relaxes back into the chair and smiles. It should be a gentle smile, but there's something there that I just don't like. A hint of arrogance, maybe? It's like a poacher's smile, just before he pulls the trigger. "If Eddie used stimulants, M-Miss Tam, then I am afraid that he kept it from me too. A-as Lori says, he wished to find employment with a major company and didn't want to ruin his chances of that happening." He coughs again, only once this time, and says, "I spoke with Eddie online a lot before his death. He told me he had met a man who was interested in hiring him, but I wasn't sure whether to believe him or not. Eddie was a good friend, but it is difficult for an Addict to become a Pro. He was *very* good with programming, though. If anyone could do it, it would be him."

"He told me that he had an interview too," Lori says, sitting up again now. The tears haven't made what little makeup she wears run, though I doubt she'd take solace in that right now. "But he didn't say who with. Did he tell you at all?"

"Hmm," Gaz replies, the sound gruffer than it should be. "He did mention something. A name. Now, what was it?" He takes in a wheezing breath and continues, "H-Hollister, I think. I am afraid that I do not remember the name of the company, though."

I nod. "We can look that up. If the net doesn't give us a clue, I'll just warrant one of the local government offices. I know that the virtual world lets people work remotely anywhere, but Pros are expected to stay in the office for the duration of their shift. If he *did* have a job interview, then they'd have to have a local branch."

"I quite agree, M-Miss Tam," he replies, and flashes that smile again.

"Well then," I say, and push to my feet. "I think that that'll do for now. If we have any further questions, can we come back to you?"

"Of course. But if you could let me know in advance next time, it would be much appreciated. I could perhaps get some refreshments ready, if that would be suitable?"

"Sure." I reach into my pocket and pull out a business card, then walk over to Gaz and hand it to him. "In the meantime, if you think of anything at all that may be useful, my details are on there."

"Thank you, M-Miss Tam. I will." He turns to Lori then and adds, "And again, my c-condolences, Lori."

"Thank you," she replies, then stands up and moves beside me. "You too."

Gaz waves cordially and says, "You will forgive me if I don't see you out. At my current speed, it may take longer to escort you to the door than it has taken you to talk to me."

"That is not a problem at all, Mr. Locke. And thank you for your time."

He nods, and we make our own way out. Once the door has clicked shut, Lori turns to me and starts to say something, but I wave to her to silence and glance back at the door. "Wait until we're back at the office," I say.

We walk the rest of the way in silence.

I PUSH MY office door shut and Lori leans herself against the wall. "There's something strange about him," she says. "I mean, I don't know if he was always like that, we didn't really speak much before, but he seemed really...off."

"Could be damage from the amount of time he spends online. You heard what he said about healthcare, right?"

"I know, I know. He just *felt* different from when I've seen him before. Sort of like he knew more than he was saying but didn't think it was possible for anyone to figure that out?"

I nod. "I do know what you mean. That's why I cut the interview short. He was the wrong sort of compliant; feeding us snippets of things, but not giving us anything too definite. It could be that he really wasn't sure about things, but there was something about the way he smiled when we started mentioning stimulants that made me feel uneasy. Honestly, that was the main reason that I left Bert there to run surveillance." I sweep the hair out of my eyes and try a smile. "Still, he did at least confirm that Eddie had an interview with Dean Hollister."

"Yeah," Lori replies, her head dropping.

I place a hand on her shoulder and she turns to look at me, the tears welling up again. "If this is too hard for you, I can go and interview Hollister myself. Or if you need a break, we can grab a drink somewhere first?"

Lori giggles quietly and snuffles her nose. "Worst timing to ask someone on a date ever."

I roll my eyes, and Lori balls her fist up and slaps it lightly across my shoulder.

She wipes her eyes with her wrist and says, "Seriously, though, I want to keep going. But once everything's done, I might *need* a drink."

I smile and tap the door. "Let's get moving then. After all, the quicker we solve the case, the quicker you get the date that you *clearly* desperately want."

Lori laughs, a little louder and little brighter this time. Honestly, I don't know if she is seriously interested in me or not. Hell, I don't really know if I'm interested in her, or if I'm just beginning to feel the loneliness again. First things first, though. I have a murder to solve.

Nineteen

IT TAKES SOME time to find out which office Dean Hollister is currently working in. Being the CEO of multiple companies means that he has to split his time between a number of locations. While he can no doubt work on the business for all six no matter what office he is in, there is obviously a need to be on hand at a specific location depending on what is being worked on at the time and what takes priority. We finally find him in the office where he held his final meeting with Eddie Redwood: the local branch of Shift Source Limited.

This particular office is where Tech Shifting began. While the public only really knows the process from its release five years ago, the files we acquired from Jeremy show that Hollister's initial foray into Shifting was two years before that. That doesn't mean much, of course; just that the process underwent two years of design and testing before it was released to the public. Given the danger aspect of the initial operation and the precision involved with suiting up, that's not surprising. These days, while Hollister still presides over things from this particular office, the brunt of the work below him appears to be split between the company's European office in Brussels and their Australasian office in Canberra. Despite this jump in location to places as far apart as Belgium and Australia, the SSL website is very quick to point out that this founding office is still the hub point for the generation and testing of new ideas. I guess that the overseas offices just provide cheaper labour for the mass-production-level grunt work.

What surprises me is the process for getting a meeting with Dean Hollister. After we found out which office he was in, I let the receptionist know that we were looking to make an appointment with him so that we could discuss Edward Redwood. As soon as that message was passed on, Hollister told the admittedly very helpful lady on the main desk to ask us to come over straightaway and he would clear his schedule. Openly inviting us to chat like that after learning that a PI was on the way caught me a little off guard.

I originally intended for Lori to stay in the car for this one. When it came to visiting her brother's house, her familiarity with the place was essential. By the same token, it made sense for her to join me in visiting Gary Locke, because being known to him worked in a lot of different ways. Aside from her own private-time activities, though, she had no connection to Dean Hollister or his various places of work. That, combined with the obvious effect that the talk with Gary had on her, made her staying outside all the more sensible an idea.

She insisted on coming in with me and wouldn't take no for an answer, so I ended up giving in far more easily than I normally would. This isn't the first time that I've had a client want to take a hands-on approach to a case, and while not always ideal, it's something that's workable if they're willing to cooperate with what you're saying. In this case, I could at least justify her being there in my head as a way to ensure that nothing too untoward would be said. If Dean Hollister mentioned something about Eddie Redwood that was unequivocally false, Lori would be able to pick up on that, whereas I would not. On top of that, the potential quick resolution and a chance to see the SSL office from the inside seemed to cheer Lori a little.

When we arrive, the receptionist I spoke to on the phone immediately buzzes for our escort. I expect a burly security guard to arrive. What we get is a friendly looking guy in a business suit who immediately becomes fascinated with Lori's plugs. While the two of them chat about Ink and how the process was for Lori, a conversation which confirms that Lori underwent the process three years ago, when her brand of plug was still new, I take note of our surroundings.

The ground floor is pretty much a carbon copy of any major office in the area; all open with one central reception point. Things seem quiet today, but you'd think that it would get pretty busy during peak business times, especially when investors or overseas staff visit. The main desk is only big enough for one person, so whoever mans it during those times must be pretty damn efficient. Given how she's been with us, I wouldn't be surprised if it is the self-same woman who's down there now. I can admire that. It almost makes me feel guilty that I didn't bother to check her name. Almost.

The elevator is nice enough. Spacious, and in our case, virtually empty. It moves quickly and smoothly, taking us up to floor twenty-two, the highest of the general work floors. The office guy—who I only know is named Mr. Ghoul, spelled like the Arabian monster but pronounced Gow-ool, because Lori has been paying more attention to what he's been saying than I have—finally grabs my attention enough to explain that there are a further ten floors below ground. Only three of the six ground-floor elevators go down that way, while the other three mirror this one and only head upwards. The floor we're now on is where a lot of the big decisions are made and passed out to the various other floors and offices. The project leads and high-end executives all occupy the place, and work tirelessly in both the real world and the virtual one.

The floor itself is what I would describe as clean-modern; the sort of look that's almost shiny white and is clearly kept that way through regular and intensive maintenance work. The effect is that, even with the occasional areas of messy cabling work and the ever-advancing technology of the day, it always looks new, and always looks professional. It's how a lot of people expect places like banks and tax offices to appear until they actually get to see one from the inside on any of the noncustomer-facing floors. The reason we've stopped here is because it's as high as this particular elevator goes. This is because security protocol states that no intruder must be able to reach the highest floor where all the important stuff is located. Like the CEO. The elevator to that office is at the other end of the floor, and the only way to get access is if either the occupant buzzes you up or you know the override codes. No one in this office other than Dean Hollister knows the override codes, so emergencies would need to be dealt with via an international effort. What this also means is that, should an armed intruder get in, the top-level staff can make their way up to the safe area quickly.

Walking across the floor, I count six banks of log-in chairs, two of which are fully occupied. Alongside these, various groups of desks house bustling, laughing staff as they go about their daily tasks. Towards the end of the floor is a corridor that we are told leads to the toilets, the relaxation areas, and the various print and comms rooms with their printers and e-fax machines. That the faxes are still needed surprises me. E-fax machines were created as a way to replace aging paper-dependent fax machines by combining them with internal e-mail systems. This meant that you could take a paper print if needed, but would not be reliant on owning hard copies of the files if you needed to send a lot; you just required a memory stick or a wireless link-up. The thinking is that, while the more recent technological developments encompass the preferred methods of doing pretty much everything, there is a tendency for a lot of these newer systems to be a little unstable. Things like the e-faxes are slower, but sturdier and less prone to the issues prevalent in their modern counterparts. As a result, most successful businesses still have some older machines in their offices, just in case.

Finally, we reach the elevator at the end of the sports-field-sized room, and Mr. Ghoul lets Dean Hollister know that we have arrived. Within seconds, our escort has ushered us inside, said his good-byes, and sent us on our merry way to the highest floor of the building.

Twenty

HOLLISTER'S SANCTUARY ON the top floor is about as close as an office can get to "stunning" for me. The room is circular and surrounded by thick-looking glass. Through the windows, an expanse of grass stretches to the guardrails that surround the outermost edges of the building. From here, I can see that the floor below extends a lot further than I thought it did, placing this particular office in the centre of the building. Glancing to my left, I can see the flag on the high-rise parking structure at the top of Northern Main Street fluttering in the breeze, which means that the top floor is higher up than it appeared too.

In the middle of the room sits a large desk, and behind this sits a man struggling to maintain a vaguely relaxed smile. He waits for us to finish taking everything in and walk towards him before he rises to meet us.

"It is a beautiful view, isn't it? The greenery was my idea. I enjoy the mix, you see. Nature looking out over where we are now as a species. I find it helps to remind me of the things that we shouldn't leave behind. Dean Hollister."

"Cassandra Tam," I say, taking his outstretched hand. His skin is clammy. That combined with the clear tenseness in his face adds up to nervousness. "And this is Lori Redwood. Is the grass real?"

"One hundred percent real, yes," he replies, offering his hand to Lori now. His suit jacket is open, and the tightness of the work shirt beneath it betrays that when he bought it, he was probably a little slimmer than he is now. Well, that or he's either deluded or just really bad at picking sizes. "Please, sit down." He waves his arm towards the two chairs at the front of his desk, then walks immediately back to his seat without waiting to see if we will do as he asks and starts sliding his computer monitor out of the way so that he can see us more easily.

"I see a monitor, but no keyboard," I say, making sure that I keep my voice conversational.

Dean Hollister sinks back into his chair and smiles, the rudimentary ice-breaking seeming to have the desired effect. He pushes his glasses back up to the bridge of his nose and flicks a section of the desk open to reveal a keyboard. "I like to keep my desk fairly clear in case a mass of paperwork comes in. I'd use a holo-monitor and keyboard, but I'm not fond of the way that they flicker. As much as I hate to admit it, at fifty-three, my eyesight is that of a seventy-odd-year-old. The flickering could be fixed fairly easily, of course, but that would invalidate our warranties and go against the terms of the deal that we have with Sun Burst LLC. I keep trying to tell their design team that simply switching to some of our light bars would create a much more stable image, but they won't have it. They just state some nonsense about breaching the barrier between customer and business partner. It's all rather silly if you ask me. Mutual back-scratching makes the world go round, or so I say."

"Cooperation," I reply. "It makes things far easier."

"Exactly. Which is why, when I heard who it was that you wished to speak about, I was so eager to speak to you. To be frank, I am surprised that the police didn't come to me before they made their decision on the case."

I shrug, noting that both Joe and L3G3ND had the same reaction when I visited them yesterday. "They took the case for what it looked like. Another VJ Addict accidentally overdosing on Flash7."

"But you don't believe that, do you, Miss Tam?"

I nod to Lori and say, "My client does not believe that. My thoughts on the case are fairly immaterial unless we find substantiating evidence to prove things one way or the other."

"Ah, but if you've come to me, then that means you know Mr. Redwood and I were holding discussions, yes?"

"Eddie said that he had a job interview with a Pro company," Lori replies. "He didn't say who with, though, so it took a while to figure out who we should speak to."

"You checked with the Monitoring Office, no doubt. Am I remembering correctly, Miss Redwood, that you are the deceased's sister?" Lori nods, and he continues, "That surprises me. Perhaps I should begin with how I came to be interviewing Mr. Redwood in the first place?"

"I think that would be best," I reply, adding the phrase "that surprises me" to my mental notebook. "It's pretty unusual for an Addict to even be considered by a Pro company, isn't it?"

"Yes, it is. Though, when I first spoke to Mr. Redwood, I was unaware that he was an Addict. You see, most people like to separate their work and private lives. For me, I am aware how much we rely on spaces such as the virtual world for business, and so I like to find ways to separate my work and private life while in the work area."

"Like you do with the grass here?"

"Exactly. There are plenty of places, even in the business-centric areas of the virtual world, where you can go to relax. Libraries, for example, or viewing bars."

"Viewing bars...That sounds familiar," I say.

"They are much like bars that you would find out here, but instead of serving drinks, they provide access to viewing screens where you can watch films, play games, or just study clips of wildlife, both current and extinct. Mr. Redwood happened to come across me in one such bar, and recognised me from a seminar that I'd run several months prior."

"May I ask what the seminar was on?"

"Joint working through multisource engagement. From what he said that first day, it really inspired him to keep pushing ahead with his goals of achieving success in the programming market. He was suitably brazen for that end of things, and wondered if I would be interested in seeing something he had been working on in relation to my own SnapDragon Suite. Are you aware of this system at all?"

"We are, yes," I reply.

"Eddie's house was full of books about SnapDragon," Lori adds. "It looked like he was reading one when he..." Her voice cracks, and tears well up again. Hollister nods solemnly, and produces a handful of tissues from his drawer, handing them straight to the grateful Lori.

"That does not surprise me," he says. "He seemed like the sort of person who would do his research before he tinkered with anything. In all honesty, despite his positive attitude, I wasn't certain that he would be able to offer me much I hadn't either seen before or already had in the pipeline. Still, I remember the frustration of not being given a shot when I was just trying to make a name for myself. It wasn't until after I'd suffered many rejections that one sympathetic entrepreneur finally gave me the opportunity to show him what I could do, purely on the off-chance that he'd stumble across something special. Knowing that was all it took to make both him and me a lot of money, I would be foolish not to allow others the same opportunities. Had he been useless, what would

I have lost, really? An hour of my day? Time can be made up, missed chances cannot. So I invited him to our offices to give me a demonstration of his work."

"You say that you met Mr. Redwood in a bar, but the logs that we obtained from the Monitoring office show that *all* the meetings you held with him in the month prior to his death were at the virtual site of your Hollister and Holtz offices. Can I assume, therefore, that the bar meeting was before that?"

Hollister sits back into his chair and drums his fingers on the desk. "I suppose it must have been. I can certainly find the precise date for you if you wish. I take the liberty of recording all conversations I have online, so the transcript of that and all the others will be stored on our servers." He pauses for a moment, then says, "I don't believe there is anything in the transcripts that would contravene either the running of this business or data protection. Once we're done, I would be happy for you to take copies of the files if that would be of assistance?"

I raise a curious eyebrow Hollister's way and say, "It would be, yes. Mr. Hollister, I'm sorry if this seems a little untoward, but you seem far too ready to offer assistance. Now, I'm sure that you are banking on the transcripts showing that you had no part in Mr. Redwood's death, but in my experience, people with nothing to hide tend to be a bit cagier than you have been."

Hollister sighs. He stands up, removes his suit jacket, hangs it on the back of his chair, and sits down again, then uses the sleeve of his work shirt to wipe the sweat from his brow.

"Miss Tam, Miss Redwood, I can assure you that I have nothing to hide. As I said before, I was surprised that the police did not come to speak to me already. It would have been a rather simple task to find out, as you have, that I spoke with Mr. Redwood, and again, as *you* have pointed out, it is unusual for an Addict to be in a position where employment by a Pro company is possible. Had I said I could have found the date and not explained how, you would have no doubt asked. When I mentioned the transcripts, you would have asked for copies. Had I then refused, you would likely slap a warrant on me and take them anyway. Though I can understand your suspicion, I simply wish to offer as much cooperation as I can in order to *clear* any suspicion that may feasibly hang over me."

"What you're saying makes sense," I reply, keeping my face neutral. "But I would not be doing my job properly if I did not consider every possibility and question things that seem odd. It may well be that everything you're telling us is true, but without the full story, we won't know that for sure."

"I understand, of course. It is much the same when testing a new product or considering a business proposal. Please try to understand my position here too, though. Regardless, shall I continue?"

"Please do."

"Mr. Redwood came to the offices as requested and brought with him a copy of his modified SnapDragon system. He told me that he had considered the possibility of it being used by law enforcement agencies, but when he had researched this, he found that no such agencies were licensed users. I asked him why he thought that might be and his response was that the systems they were known to use were able to work covertly. He had wondered why they had this feature but SnapDragon did not, and the only thing that he could come up with was that the enforcement systems tended to be less complex in nature, and so easier to work with, in terms of masking their presence.

"He was correct. The SnapDragon Suite goes far more in depth than anything the law enforcement agencies use, but it is a bulky system that would be very difficult to hide. Mr. Redwood claimed to have been able to create a masking tool that would allow SnapDragon to run undetected without losing functionality. I was, needless to say, intrigued. We set up a test whereby I installed his masking tool and tasked SnapDragon with monitoring a member of staff for five minutes, after which it was to send me a full report. We checked, multiple times, and sure enough, there was no trace of SnapDragon having been running. It was really quite incredible."

I glance to the side and see Lori smiling proudly. Good. It sounds like Eddie really was as talented as she thought, and regardless of what happens with the investigation, that's something she *should* be proud of.

"I agreed to run some more tests on his work," Hollister continues, "and invited him to come back to view the results. He leaped at the opportunity, of course, but seemed a little nervous. That was to be expected; it was a big step for him, after all. We met up again a few days later, and again a few more times after that. Eventually, I told him I was suitably impressed with his work that I was interested in bringing him on board to develop it as a Hollister and Holtz product, with a view to giving him a cut of the profits if we could convince the law enforcement agencies to take it on. But as I explained to him, there were some formalities that would need to be worked through first."

"What sort of formalities?" Lori asks, beating me to the question.

"Well, first I wanted to know why he came to me rather than going straight to the agencies themselves. It was entirely possible that he could have gained a better deal for himself by simply offering the product to them and letting them negotiate a low price with me. As it happens, he said that he had considered this but chosen the route that he did because he believed in long-term investments. As he saw it, working directly with us opened more doors and gave him the opportunity to work on other things internally while receiving company support."

Lori nods. "That's what I would have done too, I think."

"You'd be surprised how many don't," Hollister replies, shaking his head. "There are a lot of good people out there who are more interested in the next quick hit rather than looking at the future. It's a shame, really. Anyway, I pointed out that in order for us to consider him for a position we would need to run a full health test on him. I asked if there was anything we should know about, and *that* was when he mentioned that he was a VJ Addict. He was quick to add that he didn't use synth stimulants, of course, as his goal had always been Pro employment and he didn't want to ruin his chances of that. He did mention that he was worried that the amount of time that he spent online may show signs of damage, though."

"And what did you think when he said that?" I ask.

"I was surprised that he came clean, though pleasantly so. I had hoped that he would. You see, we perform background checks on potential employees as a standard, so once we knew that Mr. Redwood's work was up to scratch, I set one running before I spoke to him. The initial set of checks flag up any immediate areas for concern, and his virtual world usage levels, combined with his insistence on meeting in the virtual world rather than the real world, was a potential sign of him being an Addict. I didn't question why he didn't tell me sooner—his reasoning there would have been obvious—but that he came out with it without direct prompting was a good sign. Had he not, I may have had to terminate the offer."

"Did he submit himself to the health checks, and would I be able to get a copy of the results?"

"He did, yes, which is another reason why I was expecting the police to call. In terms of the actual results, it would be illegal for me to just hand them out—however, the transcript where we discussed them will give you a rundown. I try to be thorough where appropriate."

"The transcript may be enough, then. You say that Mr. Redwood submitting to the tests was what made you expect a police call. Can you elaborate on that?"

"It was less that he submitted to them, and more the results themselves. You see, it was public knowledge before the police came to a decision on the case, that he had died with needle in hand." He spots Lori flinch at that and smiles apologetically. "My apologies, Miss Redwood. My wording was perhaps more blunt than needed. The problem for me was that the tests came back clean. According to what we received, he had *never* used Flash7 or any other synth stimulant in his life. These were in-house tests too, not some outside agency report that could have been tampered with. After that, the idea that he overdosed was inconceivable to me. And with what happened next, I knew that I would be, or rather *should* have been, a suspect."

"What happened next, Mr. Hollister?"

"The second part of the background checks came through. That's where we apply to the Monitoring Office for searches based on certain types of activity and, if they arise, certain buzz words." He turns to look at Lori again, and asks, "Miss Redwood, were you aware that your brother was a regular contributor to a blog site?"

"A blog site? No. Blogging isn't illegal, though."

"No, in general terms, it is not. Some types of blogs can border on illegality, however. Others can also fall under the heading of 'potentially causing damage to the image of the employer. In your brother's case, he wrote for a site called *The Roots of Eden are Rotten* under the pseudonym SilverSingsLoudly. Do you know of the site at all?"

"No," Lori replies, shaking her head.

"I do," I reply. "It's a site that hosts a bunch of political and economic conspiracy theories and fallacies. You can tell which pieces on there are built purely to stir trouble and which have a shred of truth to them, though even some of those push it at times. I'm surprised that none of the authors have been held accountable for libel as yet."

"Yes, well, that's because they're very careful in how they present their postings. Simply proclaiming something a rumour and leaving a disclaimer that it may not be true is enough to avoid charges in most cases. In others, the postings are so over the top that the idea they could have a measurable impact on the target is itself quite ludicrous. In that situation, the cost of engaging in a legal battle over it would simply not be cost-effective, and I mean that in terms of both the actual monetary cost and the potential damage that you would do yourself by playing into it."

"Because to openly confront them gives the impression that you're trying to hide something," Lori replies. "It's the same in the general press. A lot of the time, challenging an article just adds fuel to the fire for whatever the original point was."

"Exactly," Hollister replies. "This, though, was a little more serious."

"Serious in what way?" I ask.

"There was a posting where the various staff were given targets, all of which they described as 'names of a high standing'. The targets were to be 'pursued voraciously in the interest of uncovering the unsavoury truth of their dealings and to reveal the extent of the damage that they have wrought upon society'. SilverSingsLoudly was given *my* name."

"And once you realised this, what did you do?"

"I confronted him with it, of course. I outright accused him of trying to gain employment in order to use his masking tool to dig for dirt and steal confidential information."

"And he denied this?"

"Not at all, no. He openly admitted that this was what he was doing and that he fully intended to 'reveal to the world, the evil that I do'."

"Evil within Hollister and Holtz?"

"Within all my companies, but in particular Shift Source Limited. Hollister and Holtz was merely a way to get his foot in the door."

I pause, suddenly aware that bringing Lori with me on this one may have been a mistake. I consider whether asking to take a break and sending Lori home would be a good idea at this point, but she speaks before I can.

"Why SSL in particular?" she asks.

Hollister looks at her, the concern on his face confirming my suspicions before he even begins to explain. "He viewed Tech Shifter technology and the popularity of it as an abomination in the eyes of God.

I do not know what religion Mr. Redwood followed, but as far as he was concerned, Tech Shifting was simply a perversion of the human form, and all those who used it were weak-minded souls that had made the choice to fall into temptation. Temptation offered by a demon named Dean Hollister."

"That...that can't be right..." Lori whispers.

"You remember I said it surprised me that you are Mr. Redwood's sister? That was not because you are a Tech Shifter. Knowing that of you, and knowing his views on the matter, adds some logic to what he attempted. What surprised me was that you were a Tech Shifter and yet you were pursuing his death because you seem to want some form of justice for him. Can I assume that he never spoke to you about any of this?"

Lori shakes her head. The movement is jerky, and her eyes are wide with shock.

For his part, Hollister looks genuinely remorseful and sympathetic when he says, "Then I am sorry to be the one to tell you this. Can I get you anything? A drink, perhaps?"

Lori shakes her head again and looks at Hollister with a strange sternness in her expression. "It doesn't matter what he thought of my life choices, or what he chose to write about online. If he was murdered, I *will* find out who did it."

Hollister smiles then, and his face lights up with admiration. "I quite agree, Miss Redwood. Murder is murder, regardless of the victim. That you can set yourself on this path despite today's revelations is an admirable quality."

"Mr. Hollister," I say, trying to draw the attention away from Lori so that she can have a chance to take this all in. "When you confronted Mr. Redwood, was that the final time you met with him?"

"Yes," he replies.

"And when you discovered that he wrote for the blog site, did you learn of any of the real names of the other contributors?"

"No, though I did mention some of the IP addresses to him. That was more of a way to show that we *could* delve further into it if he left us in a position where we had to."

"And would the IP addresses be in the transcripts?"

"The ones that I mentioned, yes, though not all the ones that we traced."

"Okay," I say. I reach into my trouser pocket and pull out a small memory stick. I make a real effort to keep at least one with me at all times now, as there have been too many instances where I could have done with one and not had one with me. The Monitoring Office won't allow me to supply my own, but that's less because they make a profit on their physical media charges, and more protection against infiltrating software being saved on them. If you believe the conspiracy theorists, hacking that particular mess of systems would make you a Virtual World Deity. "If you don't mind, I'd like to copy the transcripts now. May I ask, has this meeting been recorded too?"

He nods. "I am afraid so. This is a standard security procedure, however, and one employed in many different areas of business."

"Oh, I have no problem with it," I clarify. "I simply thought that it would be useful to have a copy of today's transcript too if that would be okay?"

"Certainly," he replies, and starts tapping away on his keyboard. "Is there somewhere in particular that I should send it?"

I pull a business card from my pocket and slide it across the table. "My details are on there."

"Thank you," he says, taking the card. He reaches into one of the outside pockets of the suit jacket and pulls out his wallet, places the card inside, and slips it back into the pocket again. "If you'd like to pass the memory stick, I'll move the files across."

"It's locked by my fingerprint, I'm afraid," I say, showing him the thumb slot at the top of the casing. "I'll need to unlock it myself."

"That's fine," he replies, standing up. "The connectors are just under the desk, directly below the keyboard. SnapDragon monitors our systems anyway, so I'll be able to see if you copy anything other than the files from the folder on screen."

"I'd expect no less," I reply, walking carefully around the desk. "Out of interest, Mr. Ghoul downstairs said that the plugs my client uses were new three years ago. Is there anything that she should look out for in terms of wear and tear?" Lori glances at me in confusion, and I give her a quick raising of the eyebrows. I just hope she understands that I want her to play along.

Lori blinks and seems to catch my drift, as she says, "Actually, yeah. I try to take care of them with the recommended cleaning and oiling products, but you can never be sure if you're doing enough."

"Hmm," Hollister replies, stroking his chin. "Is your suit animal or hybrid?"

"Animal," she says. "My worry was that it takes three or four attempts to unlock the front legs these days. I just wasn't sure if the problem was with the locks or the plug interface."

"Well, I can certainly check that easily enough," he says, striding around the desk. "Do you mind if I take a look? If this is a plug problem, it will be the first one on the back of the neck."

"Sure," Lori replies, and turns the chair, making sure that Hollister's back will be to me. *Well played, Miss Redwood.*

While Hollister occupies himself with Lori, I start the files copying and slide my hand carefully into his jacket pocket. When I take it back out again, his wallet comes with it. Thankfully, it's a button front, not Velcro, so I manage to open it up and flick to the card section without any noticeable noise. I slip my phone out of my pocket and snap a quick shot of the bank card at the top, then flick through to make sure that there are no others. Luckily, he seems to be the sort who has obeyed the tax office recommendations of holding one account rather than twenty. Their thinking was publicised as being a way to simplify your tax affairs, but most people took it as them saying 'please don't make it more complicated for us to check your figures'. Whatever the reason, his only holding one card here is a good sign. I get the wallet shut and back in the pocket just as he finishes his check of Lori's plugs.

"There aren't any obvious physical faults here," he says. "And usually, an internal fault results in the physical plug getting burnt too. How long have you had the issue?"

"A few months," Lori replies.

"In that case, I would think that the issue is with the locking mechanism on the suit. What sort of animal is it?"

"A panther. I went for the black colouring, if that helps?"

"Ah, she sounds beautiful. I always did like the big cat designs. Unfortunately, the locking issue is quite common in them. I tell you what. I do feel bad for the pain you've gone through, especially that which I have added. As a one-off, I would be happy to provide a full maintenance check for you and your suit, free of charge, with our head tech team."

"Thank you," she says. "I will have to decline for now, though, at least until I know whether you *did* have anything to do with Eddie's death."

Hollister smiles kindly and replies, "I understand. The offer will remain open indefinitely."

Lori nods and looks to me. I pull the memory stick from the connection point, and stand up. "Well, that's it. Thank you for your time, Mr. Hollister. It's been a useful experience."

"No, no," he replies, his voice the definition of affability. "Thank you for taking the time to listen to my side of things. It is a weight off my shoulders to know that things are in hand and that I don't have to feel like I'm hiding anything anymore. For what it's worth, I was genuinely impressed with Mr. Redwood's skill, and was sad to see things end the way they did. Even if he hadn't died, it was such a waste of a brilliant mind. If he *was* murdered, I truly hope that you catch the person responsible."

"As do we," I reply. "If you remember anything that may be of use, please do get in touch. And in the meantime, if we have any more questions, will you be fine for us to contact you again?"

"I will, and of course."

"Oh, one more thing," I add. "Mr. Ghoul pointed out that you have some e-fax machines. It's cheeky to ask, but would you object if I used one quickly? An associate of mine has been out of town questioning another person of interest for the case, and said that he had a summary of his interview for me. Rather than wait to meet up, would you possibly consent to allowing him to send it here for me?"

"Of course," he replies. "I shall let Mr. Ghoul know to let you have access to the comms rooms."

We all repeat our thank-yous and shake hands like we've just closed a business deal, and both Lori and I make our way back to the elevator. Once we're safely inside, I pull out my phone and type out a quick message: *The elevator is probably full of recording devices too, so don't speak. What I'm about to do is slightly illegal. I need you to head down to the car and leave this one to me.*

I hold the phone out to Lori. She reads the message and nods.

Once we come out on the next floor down, Mr. Ghoul is already waiting for us. He shows me to the comms area and, at my request, the toilets, then escorts Lori back towards the elevator at the other end of the room, temporarily leaving a colleague, Mr. Mackintosh, to wait with me.

Twenty-One

THE E-FAX MACHINE is across the hall and around the corner from the toilets, and is not only so bulky that you can't miss it, it also has a convenient laminated sheet of paper stuck to the wall above it, confirming the number for incoming messages. I take note of that by setting it as the filename for the photo of Hollister's bank card, and explain to the almost annoyingly cheery Mr. Mackintosh that I'll give my colleague a call while I freshen up and have him send the files over. I ask if, just in case they come while I'm still finishing up, Mr. Mackintosh would be willing to wait by the machine for me, and he's more than happy to oblige. I'd say that security here was lax, but in all honesty, there's very little obvious damage that I could do where I'm going. The company won't have done anything stupid like put the main servers in the ladies' washrooms, and to get back to the main office, I would have to pass by the comms rooms anyway.

With my office shadow happily seconded to the role of what is essentially "mail duty for a visitor", I push open the washroom door and walk inside. Dean Hollister giving every impression of being the law-abiding sort, I'm not surprised to find the "cleaning in progress" stands tucked neatly in the corner of the spacious room. Is he really as clean as he puts across? We'll soon find out.

A quick check of the three stalls shows that this particular washroom is empty. Satisfied that this will suit my needs, I pick up the safety stand and carefully prop it up outside the main door. With two other ladies' washrooms just a little further down the hall, both no doubt identical to this one, no one is likely to drop in if it looks like the cleaner has arrived.

Certain that my privacy is now guaranteed, I flip open my phone and check the name of the bank on Hollister's bank card. *New Hopeland First National.* A quick internet search brings up their customer services number and lets me dial straight through. There was a time that dialling a general number like this would result in a lengthy wait on hold, but modern advances in thinking have allowed managers to see what should have been obvious in the first place. If both your staff and the general public say that long hold times are symptomatic of understaffing in call centres, then that probably *is* the problem. As a result, most companies now have three times as many call handlers as they used to. While this obviously helps with keeping the time people spend on hold pretty low, it doesn't address the issue of poor training for staff. For that, however, I am grateful. If I thought for one minute that I was about to get a competent, well-trained person to deal with, then this would be a stupid idea. After less than thirty seconds, the cheesy royalty-free music cuts and the bustle of a busy call centre crackles in over the line.

"Good afternoon, caller, this is NHFN, and you're speaking to Steve. Can I take your name and account number please?"

"Hi, Steve," I reply, moving myself into a stall and placing the phone on speaker. I continue talking while I scroll the screen back to the photo of Hollister's bank card, doing the best I can to mask my accent with a poor man's imitation of a New York edge. "I'm afraid it's not my account that I'm calling about."

"I see. Ordinarily, we would be required to speak to the account holder, but if they're there at all, I would be willing to accept their verbal consent to speak to you on a one-off basis."

"Now, Steve, if my boss were available to talk, don't you think that he'd be calling himself?"

"In that case, I'm not sure if I'll be able to help at all. May I ask what the query is in relation to?"

"Basically, my boss was concerned that the security of his account may have been compromised. The problem is, there's a bit less in there than he was expecting, but 'cause he uses the account for both business and personal stuff, he thought it may just be that he bought something and forgot about it. He did try the online account, but he's having some connection issues at the moment. Something about his virus software and a false positive?"

"I see. Well, we certainly don't like to think that our customers are suffering hardship through any potential faults in our security systems. Unfortunately, though, without the account holder's permission, I won't really be able to confirm anything to you."

"I understand that, but he is going to be so mad at me if I come back to him with nothing. Isn't there anything that you can do? I'm already on a warning for screwing up the drinks at the last board meeting, and I *really* don't want to lose another job," I plead, then allow myself a smile at the uncomfortable silence at the other end of the line.

"Uhm...I'm sorry, but did you confirm your name?"

"No, sorry, that's my fault. It's Miss Gow-ool, spelt G-H-O-U-L."

"Like the ghost thing?"

"Demon, but yes."

"Okay, Miss Ghoul. We really do take security seriously here, and protocol simply won't allow me to just give you details for another person over the phone without their express consent. I'm sorry, but I'm not sure what I can do for you here."

"Okay," I reply, keeping my tone downtrodden. I throw in a few sobs and sniffles for added emphasis, and Steve inhales sharply at the other end of the line.

"Miss Ghoul? Are you okay?"

"Yes," I squeak. "It's just...if you could..." I pause, gasp, and exclaim, "That's it! With business accounts, do you keep a list of office contact details on record, or could you check the location of a machine if I were to give you...maybe an e-fax number?"

"We do keep numbers on file, yes, but that doesn't change that I would be unable to respond to you, only the account holder."

"That's what I mean, though. I'm in a different office to my boss right now, but I could give you the e-fax number for the building that he's in and you could mark the correspondence for his attention. It would be passed straight to him via our internal system."

"That...would work," he says, his voice uncertain. "But in that case, wouldn't an e-mail be more secure?"

"That was part of his worry. He thought that the security breach, if there was one, may have come from someone hacking into his account and copying his details from the last statement that you sent. With the e-fax, it's a physical copy so he can just grab it and not have to worry."

"That makes sense, I guess. I mean, what sort of information did he want?"

"Nothing too major, just a statement covering the last two months. The only extra he wanted on it was a list of payment origins for money going out."

"So IP addresses, cheque numbers, phone numbers for telephone transfers, that type of thing?"

"That's right. Please, Steve, I really don't want to get in trouble again."

Steve sighs heavily and gives in. "Okay, okay, I think that should be alright. Have you got your boss' details there with you?"

"Thank you," I reply, laying on the gratitude and relief in thick measures. "Thank you so much. Yes, I have them here."

Twenty-Two

I RUN THROUGH Hollister's details pretty quickly, and Steve runs a quick check of the e-fax number against the contact details held on the business end of the account. Once he's confirmed that matches, he loads up the files and I make my way out of the washroom, phone now switched back to normal mode and held up to my ear on a low volume. I make it back to the e-fax machine just as he finishes his checks.

"So that's all the details for the last two months, right?"

"Yes," he says. "I'll just hit send now...and done."

"Thank you so much, Steve, you're a lifesaver."

The e-fax machine springs noisily into life, but Steve doesn't seem to notice it. "You're welcome, Miss Ghoul. Is there anything else I can help you with?"

"No, no, that was it. Thanks again."

"You're welcome. Have a good day."

I hang up and grab the papers as they start to come through. A quick glance shows that they are indeed the details I requested. From the look of it, each month runs to about fifteen pages, which isn't surprising if we're assuming that *all* business and private expenditure goes through the one account.

"Sorry," I say to Mr. Mackintosh, grabbing the final sheet. "I didn't realise there'd be so much. Steve is pretty thorough, though."

"Not a problem, Miss Tam. Now, if you'd like to come this way, I'll get you back to the main desk."

I smile politely and follow along like an obedient little guest. I could have pointed out that I could happily find my own way back, and there have been some days where I'd have said just that just to get a rise out of him, but today at least I'd rather avoid conflict. I soon find myself outside the building and getting back into Lori's car. Lori looks about as happy as I'd expect after the talk with Hollister.

"So what did you do?" she asks.

"Got a copy of his bank statements for the last two months. If he paid Devin to murder Eddie, it'll be in here."

"Unless he used a different account."

"Yeah. He looked like he at the very least puts on a front of being big on following the letter of the law, though, and he seems to value the input of others, so…" I wave the wad of papers and add, "From the amount of info they sent me, I reckon he'll have taken the single account advice from the tax office as gospel."

Lori starts the car up and we head out of the parking lot. "So, do you think that he did it?"

"Like I said before, he has the means. We can find out if Eddie really did write for the blog easily enough, and if that turns out to be true, then Hollister has a motive too. Whether that means he really is hiding something in one of the companies remains to be seen. *The Roots of Eden are Rotten* are hardly reputable for giving whole truths, so it could just be the betrayal or a fear that they'd make something up that hit a little too close to home."

"It seems weird that he just gave us all that, though. He's smart."

"That'd be why he gave it to us. Guilty people are expected to hide what they did, but they don't always do it how you'd think, if at all. He'd know that what he told us puts him in the picture as far as having a motive goes, so he could be banking on us thinking that his info dump was too obvious to pursue. What he told us could be untrue, or it could be littered with half-truths. Or, he may be entirely innocent and telling the complete truth. We won't know for certain just yet."

"So what happens now?"

"Now, you drop me back home so that I can go through these, and you head back to yours to get some rest."

"But…" she begins, but I cut her off.

"No, Lori. This is going to take me a while, 'cause I'm gonna have to do it all manually. You've had a hard enough day as it is, and whatever answers this gives us are just going to make it harder. Rest now so that you can deal with whatever happens later."

Lori sighs, and we spend the rest of the journey in silence.

Twenty-Three

I INTENDED TO recall Bert once I got home, but the more I thought about the amount of work that lay ahead, the easier it became to convince myself that a little more surveillance of Gary Locke might be useful. I love him to bits, but Bert has an awful habit of making a nuisance of himself when it comes to paperwork. That'll be his tendency to get bored creeping in. There's not much duller than watching someone else pore over masses of really boring data. No, he'll enjoy the job more than being here—well, if enjoy's the right word. Can Familiars really enjoy anything? Their responses are programmed and learned over time, but that's not too far removed from a growing child learning the appropriate way to respond to...I shake my head. My subconscious is finding ways to distract me from the task at hand. *Bad Cassandra*, I admonish myself. *Just get on with it.*

If Dean Hollister was a normal person rather than one of the rich and powerful, finding a fee the size that Devin normally charges among his outgoings would be easy, but a lot of the business procurements that go through his account are pretty large. I scan down the numbers on my tablet screen, leaving my thumb pressed tightly under the account number that I'm checking. Devin has six accounts that I know of, two that I found myself during investigations and four that I've learned about through working with the PD. The problem is, with Hoover being forced to pull support on this one, I won't be able to check if he has any new ones that they know about without getting one or more of the good guys in trouble. If I'd thought there was any chance that the case would blow up like it has, I'd have asked when I was applying for the warrants, just in case. *Way to go, hindsight; never useful and always a pain.*

No match, but that's not a surprise. I've got to check all the payments, 'cause I don't want to miss something stupid, but the likelihood of Devin charging something as specific as thirty-seven thousand, six hundred and ninety-three dollars and forty-three cents is remote at best. The next few entries are smaller, by which I mean they each about equal my monthly income on a good month, and judging by the recipient names probably fall under the "business premises maintenance expenditure" bracket. After that comes some genuinely small private expenditure for films, food, and clothing. I can probably skip the recipient names for anything on here below fifteen thousand dollars. After that, anything could be a Devin Carmichael account under some fake name.

I finish the first month and rub my eyes, painfully aware that the orange glow creeping in through the bedroom door means that the sun is setting. With a grunt, I push to my feet and slouch into the kitchen. The time on the tablet says 20:58, which means that it's taken me an hour and a half to check through the first half of the paperwork. I fill the kettle and flick it on, then lean back against the counter and cross my arms. *Let's see…*Unless Devin is using another account, this means that either Hollister didn't have any long-term plan to kill Eddie Redwood, or he didn't pay Devin at all. Or Hollister has another account. The second half of the paperwork covers the entire last month, so I can safely ignore everything after the day that Lori found Eddie's body. With Devin, it's pay first, kill second. Good. That means it should only take another forty-five minutes to get through the initial run-through. Then, if there's still no sign of a payment to Devin in there, I can start a second run-through in case I missed something. If that comes up empty, then I can start working on just using the payment origins in case there's something in there that looks out of place. People often say things had a tendency to be more efficient way back when we didn't rely on tech so much. I like to think of myself as a pretty intelligent person, and I defy anyone to find fault in my work ethic, but looking at how much of a struggle this is, I don't have a clue how people got anything done in a decent amount of time when they had to do damn near everything manually. Here's to you, office workers of the pre-twenty-first century. You have my pity.

The kettle clicks off, and I pour myself an uncharacteristically black coffee. At this point, I'm expecting a dead end with this first run of checks. If I'm right, sleep is not something I'll be getting, so a good, hard caffeine kick now is a reasonable precautionary measure. If nothing turns up at all, then Lori and I are going to need to have a long chat about what to do next. With one warrant remaining, I *could* force Hollister to provide details of *all* bank accounts held in the last two months, including any that he closed. If that comes up blank too, then we're out of fair means and down to foul in terms of gathering information. We'd also be left with Gary Locke as the only potential suspect or lead.

Right now, I could kill Inspector Bergesson for tightening the leash on Hoover like he did. *Leash. I know that I joked about "walkies" with Lori, but I wonder if Plain Jane ever takes Murphy for…*

"Ugh," I groan. "I hate paperwork. Hate it." I slap my cheeks in an effort to snap myself out of the tedium-induced attempt at sidetracking.

No more distractions, my inner voice says. *Get on with it.*

"Yes, ma'am," I grumble in reply.

I sit back into the chair at the head of my work table and take a big grimace-inducing mouthful of sadly milk-free wake-up juice. I slide the last couple of sheets of paper off to the side, stopping on the sixth from the back. Right at the top, the last payment made on the day that Lori found her brother's body. Twenty-three thousand dollars dead-on, just about in time to be viable, and not made payable to any well-known firm and company. Wouldn't it be a lucky coincidence if that's the payment to blow the case wide open? Let's just check the account number against the list and…no match.

"Diu." I sigh and flick back to the front page. First large entry, nineteen thousand dollars and eighteen cents. No match. Seventeen thousand dollars and fifty-three cents. No match. Thirty-seven thousand dollars, no match. Fifteen thousand and one dollars, no match. I tap my fingernails against the table and take another mouth of tar. What I need is a way to narrow these figures down. I could start with just the round numbers, but I'm more likely to miss something that way. Charlie only takes cash payments too, so it's not like she could just tell me what account Devin was using. Hell, even if he had paid for the stimulants via a card transaction, he'd have probably moved the money from one account to another, several times over a prolonged period of time to lengthen the trail. He could even have transferred only small amounts and made separate withdrawals…

My eyes go wide, and realisation dawns on me. I let my face slump onto the pile of papers and groan. "I am such an idiot."

Devin takes payment first and kills second. His bill would have included expenses, and his expenses would have included the cost of the Flash7. Which means that I already know the last day that he could have taken payment, and I know how much he would have been paid on top of the kill fee. I slide my chair out, the loud scraping adding to the already plentiful mass of white scratches on the hardwood floor. The marks around the table are mostly my doing, but Bert can take the blame for most of the ones everywhere else.

I make my way into the bedroom and slide open the top drawer of the filing cabinet closest to the window. The drawer is labelled as *Currently Working*, but with the amount of crap in there, a more accurate description would be *Can't Be Bothered To Tidy*. Still, being the last thing that I dumped in there, Charlie's list is at least at the top and easy to find.

I make my way back to the desk and turn the pages until I find the pink highlighted entry for Devin. The stimulants cost three thousand, two hundred dollars and sixty-seven cents. Unless prices have skyrocketed, Charlie charged him a good 50 percent more than she would most people. I guess she would have known that it was likely for a murder, so she was probably just trying to make as much money on it as possible. Assuming she did know roughly what it would be used for, I wonder if she felt any guilt. Regardless of which way her moral compass points these days, it's the sixty-seven cents that makes me smile. VJ Dealers generally charge in round sums, but Charlie liked to add the odd couple of cents on every now and then if she was a little short for the milk or whatever. No one ever asked for it to be included in the general pot because it would be a pain to split it, and she's always been one of their top sellers, so she just kinda got away with it. Once, she added two cents exactly 'cause she wanted to buy me a new tie, and she loved making the cashiers at the high-end clothing stores count out the small change.

Now, which tie was that?

I slap my cheeks again and force myself to take a swig of coffee. "Focus," I groan to myself. I trace down the numbers with my finger and find a couple of payments ending in sixty-seven cents. The first is to settle a bill of fifty-one dollars and sixty-seven cents at a well-known supermarket. In other words, not Devin. The second one is for twenty-two thousand, two hundred dollars and sixty-seven cents. That would make the kill fee nineteen thousand. That sounds about right. The recipient name is Tad Haulage Limited, which just sounds fake to me. The account number...We have a match! I throw my fist in the air and pull it back in triumph, cracking my elbow against the table in spectacular fashion in the process. I let out an involuntary whimper and grip my arm in towards my chest.

You know what? I don't care. I don't care about the pain or that I could have found this much sooner and saved myself a lot of time and effort. I don't care that I'll still have to go through the old audio transcripts to flesh the case out, or that I can add the transcript of the meeting from earlier today to that pile 'cause Hollister got it through to me about an hour ago. I don't care, 'cause the account number matches, and that means we're a whole bunch of steps closer to proving that Dean Hollister hired Devin Carmichael to kill Eddie Redwood.

The bank statement has an IP address next to the figure, which means that it was a regular banking transfer made online, whether on a real-world connection or a virtual world session. It's in the new style too, with a heavy mix of letters and numbers, which means that if it wasn't a local location, it was in another of the new-build cities. That narrows it down a lot in terms of looking for links relating to the location and the suspect. I'm hoping it'll be local, as my last warrant will still hold that way.

First things first, though. Let's dig a little deeper. There's something off about the IP address attached to the payment. The vast majority of the amounts going out seem to stem from a handful of locations, and it's pretty easy to guess what each of them relates to. This one stands out because I can't see any other incidences of it appearing during this, or the next and previous few pages. But it should still show up on the log-in reports that the Monitoring Office gave me. If I can get a match for Hollister around the time of the payment, then that would give me enough to at least tell Lori that we're pretty certain it was him.

I swipe down the top bar on the tablet and tap the local system icon. A few seconds pass before the room speakers say, "Synch to local system complete. Please state your desired settings."

"Single room audio. Tracking mode target, Cassandra Tam."

Beep. "Settings active."

"Document content search, server six, target primary folder, open case files. Subfolder, Redwood Lori. Search term, thirteen, a, dot, c, a, one hundred and seventy, dot, sixteen, dot, forty-nine, b, b, a. Full matches only, no partial matches."

"Processing," the speakers reply.

I could ask the system to search Dean Hollister's log-on history too, but given how slow it's running, that would probably just overload it.

"This is gonna take a while." I sigh and walk back to the kitchen. I pour another coffee and, this time, allow myself the luxury of milk. Hey, this is as close to case-closed as I thought I was when I believed Eddie accidentally OD'd. My diligence has earned me a reward and a chance to relax a little.

Rather than sit on my hands while I wait for my system to finish its leisurely stroll through my files, I grab my tablet, load up the notepad, and slide the stylus out from the side of the machine. I'd use the audio dictation feature, but that would present two problems.

First, until I get around to getting this thing fixed, that would put just enough strain on the system to slow it down further. Worse yet, on the last occasion I tried running dictation at the same time as a document contents search, the search crashed and the system couldn't tell me because it was having so much trouble trying to translate my ramblings into the written word. The voice recognition can understand me just fine as long as I make a point of speaking clearly, but once I get going, my accent becomes more prominent and it struggles.

Problem number two is that part of what I want to do is a five-bar gate. The audio dictation is perfectly capable of doing this, or so the instruction manual said. I, on the other hand, am not capable of remembering all the keywords and commands to make it work. Sure, I could look it up in the manual, but in this world of tech-focused advances, there is no hard copy, only a file stored on the tablet. Do I want to keep switching between the notepad and the manual every time I forget how to change where the marker goes? Do I want to risk the system deciding that having multiple files open at once, and frequently switching between the two, is the straw that broke the available-resource camel's back? Do I want to forget where I'm up to in the hard copy printouts while I'm busy messing around and most likely swearing at a machine that can't even come close to comprehending how angry I am with it?

No, no, and no. I'll go old-school and use the stylus.

I flick back to the start of the papers and note down IP addresses as I come to them, then under that, I write the type of purchase the address has been used to make. Not needing too much detail for this, I keep the headings broad: groceries, industrial purchase, private expenditure, that sort of thing. As I come across each purchase, I put a mark next to the relevant heading. It's a simple system, but it gives me a chance to see what patterns emerge.

Half an hour later, I finish triple-checking my notes. If the system takes much longer, I'm gonna have to assume it's crashed and reboot it. Okay, so there are a lot of files to go through now that I've added in all the transcripts and monitoring office data, but this is getting ridiculous. It's running like it did when I thought that one of my servers had been compromised and I had to move everything to a new one. It turned out I'd just left a couple of things running in the background without realising, causing a major slowdown and recreating a lag that I was led to believe was symptomatic of multiple users accessing the files. And so I no longer play games on my tablet.

I'll give it until I finish with these. I scroll to the top of the notepad file.

Dean Hollister only seems to use one convenience store for food shopping during the day; a local place called Jensen's Essentials that sits just off from the industrial estate. I know the place pretty well. It's a good old-fashioned mom-and-pop place with only one till. Given that, it's pretty clear that IP address 17C.BBA193.25.39AAC belongs to that particular store. As does the right to claim that it has the best fresh-made pastries this side of the Canadian border.

Online shopping at branded sites all originate from 17C.ACD998.16.16DDA, so it's most likely that belongs to his home address. If we're working with the idea that he only has one account, it would also mean that he doesn't do personal shopping during work hours, which makes him far more job focused than pretty much anyone else I've ever met.

The purchases aimed at tech supply retailers are spread across four—no, five IP addresses, which I'm assuming are his offices. It looks like there's a crossover between the stores used and the real-world addresses the purchases were made from, but that's not unexpected. He runs multiple companies, so probably just places himself in the office where he's most needed at the time. That doesn't prevent him working on things related to one of the others while he's there. It just puts him on hand to deal with specific projects.

There are a couple of items that come out from the same IP address, around the same time each month, and with no variance in price over both months. Utility bills, tax payments, and a couple of, ahem, *specialist* website subscriptions. Those will be direct debits, which means that the IP address likely relates to the bank's servers.

Unless I'm missing something, 13A.CA170.16.49.BBA only appears once, and has only been used to pay Devin.

"Search complete," the room speakers say. "One full match."

"Read match and associated address."

"IP Address: Thirteen, a, dot, c, a, one hundred and seventy, dot, sixteen, dot, forty-nine, b, b, a. Address: 17 Cornick Crescent."

"But that's…" I narrow my eyes and save a copy of the notepad file to Lori's case file. "Computer," I continue, heading to the kitchen to refill my mug. No milk this time, we're back in black, thanks to my jumping the case-closing gun. "Open folder, server six, open case files. Subfolder, Redwood Lori."

The tablet screen flickers and Lori's case file opens up. I double-tap the additional file folder that Jeremy was kind enough to supply, and open up the in-depth results relating to Eddie Redwood's last month of virtual world log-ins. One tap of the search bar and a quick flurry of touch screen key presses later, and I have a set of nice little links to the "equipment used" entries running down the side of the screen. It doesn't take long to confirm that Eddie exclusively logged in from his home address and on one headset only.

I copy the make and model and load up a web search, pasting that into the bar and adding both "tech spec" and "locking" as additional search terms. The company site for the model confirms what I thought: Eddie's headset *is* locked by retinal scan as standard.

Going back, I tap the "news" portion of the search engine and change my additional search terms to "retinal scan" and "hacked". The results don't show any cases where Eddie's model has been successfully tampered with. In fact, the only news reports relating to that specific model are a mix of favourable expert reviews and a couple of interviews with the project lead that created it.

The interviews aren't really interviews in the truest sense of the word; they're press conference quotes dressed up to run like an interview. Security seems to be the primary topic. Apparently, the team "wanted to avoid a repeat of the unfortunate incident that Mr. Morozov fell victim to."

Another quick search reveals that Mr. Mihael Morozov, CEO for the Belarusian financial advice company Маразоў і Кінгслі, translated as Morozov and Kingsley, used one of the previous models of the headset and suffered a "large financial loss" as a result of someone within his company hacking the retinal scanner. There are a couple of nice screenshots of the tools used, and a helpful caption confirming that they're all things you would find in any office or warehouse to complete modern tech projects. The hacker, a Miss D Salisbury, was arrested and charged not only with unlawfully tampering with personal equipment, but with...publishing the personal details of the victim, including the contents of several private files, on *The Roots of Eden are Rotten*, a blog site to which she was a regular contributor.

I lean back into my chair. *Hollister would have the tools, and he did point us to* Roots, *but is this all a little too neat?* "Computer, advanced document content search, server six, open case files. Subfolder, Redwood Lori, subfolder, Virtual Monitoring Data. Search Edward Redwood log in date 17 August and store time as criteria, cross-reference with log-in time for Dean Hollister on the same date."

"Processing."

I close my eyes and try to let things fall into place. *Eddie logged in for the last time and stayed in one place. That's not normal for an accidental OD. Devin could have knocked him out, but that would have automatically logged him out. Even the older headsets had that fail-safe in place. Drug-induced paralysis, maybe? But that would have shown up in the tox report that found the Flash7. Unless the PD knew it was Devin, and they wanted to hide his identity...No, Hoove was definitely surprised that Devin was involved, so unless Corporal Devereux was hiding it from him too, this wasn't a cover-up.*

"Search complete."

That was bizarrely quick. Maybe there's hope for the thing yet. "Show results on screen and save to new subfolder, folder title, comparison."

"Processing...complete."

I pick up the tablet and scan over the data. Dean Hollister logged out of the Virtual World ten minutes before Eddie logged in for the last time. He was in the head offices for Gallant Engineering. Looking at the address, Gallant Engineering is a good forty minutes away from the SSL offices, and in the opposite direction to Eddie's place.

That means there was no way that Dean Hollister could have been at Eddie's house when the payment was made. I pick up the papers that Charlie gave me and walk back into my bedroom. I slide open the *Currently Working* drawer, and chuck them in.

Outside, I can hear some guys shouting. Out of habit, I pull the drawstring and close the blinds, then split two slats with my fingers and glance out. Two guys, street clothes, angry. Probably drunk. They'll either wander off to a bar or get moved on by one of the local patrols soon, I'm sure...And there they go now, back towards the town. I can't help thinking there was something vaguely familiar about them. Maybe Lori and I tore into them on our way to Eddie's earlier. Sidestepping around the bed, I move to the other side of the window and split the blinds again, but the two men are long gone.

"That's not the mystery you're trying to solve," I remind myself. "Stop stalling."

I walk back to the desk and drop myself into the chair. *I wonder...*

"Computer. Document content search. Same initial criteria, but cross-reference with log-in time for Gary Locke or Carl Sanders on the same date."

"Processing...please wait."

"And we're back to normal," I grumble, and the door to my office explodes into the room.

Twenty-Four

THE SOUND OF the door being blown off its hinges sends a loud ringing through my ears, knocking me off balance enough to topple me from the chair, dragging the paperwork with me. It also kicks my brain into gear, and I realise how little attention I was paying after I pulled the blinds. Two guys. One with fuzzy black hair, one with short ginger spikes. The matching fake tans, dirty white vest tops, and cut-off jean shorts. The two men outside the building weren't drunks, they were the Paloma Brothers.

I scuttle to the side the moment I hit the floor, coming to my feet just as a bullet hits the space a couple of inches short of where I was. The aim was poor, but the *bam* of the gunshot rattles through my skull loud enough to leave me shaky. I keep moving, circling around the couch just as the two men strut their way into the room. The only positive to my realisation as to who I'm up against is that the Paloma Brothers are supposed to be a lot easier to deal with than some of the other heavies that you could come across in the city.

They move quickly through the residual smoke from whatever they used to blow the door and spread out, one swinging his gun towards me, and the other backing up to the wall with his own gun in hand but not raised. I drop to the floor, landing behind the couch just as another poorly aimed bullet flies into my wall. I wonder how many more lucky misses I'll get before they remember how to aim? And would it really hurt them to use silencers?

These two must be the eighth or ninth different version of the pairing that I've seen. The Paloma Brothers are essentially a codename for two hired thugs sent out by one of the local underground bosses. They're rarely actually related, and no one even bothers to pretend that they are anymore. The reason there have been so many different versions of them is that they tend to get themselves killed a lot. Their boss, Allen Fuerza, isn't anywhere near as big-time as he likes to let on, and his two-man group of crack hitmen are often just random guys that he's found on the street. Anyone in the know is aware that they're a joke as an organisation. Even then, two guys with guns and, apparently, explosives, are better prepared than one lady who stupidly left her own gun in the bedroom and her Familiar in another building.

I grab the first thing that comes to hand, an old vase that I found in a box someone left outside the door one day, and pop up just long enough to throw it at Paloma Number One. He raises his gun hand to block it, but before I can move, the ginger-haired Paloma Number Two raises his gun and takes aim, causing me to duck back again, dropping to all fours a fraction of a second before he pulls the trigger.

The *bam* of the gun is followed immediately by footsteps moving quickly from the back wall to the door side of the couch. So much for an escape route. I hop my legs up, bringing my toes flat to the floor, and launch myself forward, tackling Paloma Number Two. The impact isn't enough to take him off his feet, but I manage to barrel him back-first into the kitchen counter. He grunts loudly, drops the gun to one hand, and makes a grab for my throat. I grip him around his waist and throw myself to the floor, twisting as I go. It isn't any sort of well-practiced MMA throw, and it sure as hell isn't pretty, but it drags Number Two down hard enough to audibly knock the air out of him. I use my near hand to rip the gun from his loosened grip, but before I can aim it, he swings his other hand across, swiping my fingers and sending the weapon spinning across the room. I throw a fist into his face and wince. Okay, so it bounced the back of his head off the floor like I'd intended, but I'm pretty sure that I've broken a finger, or at least a knuckle, with that one.

I look up just in time to see Paloma Number One raise both hands and start to take a slow but careful aim at my head. Somewhere at the back of the room, the bedroom window smashes, and a high-speed ball of silver skids through into the three-part main room.

Without stopping, it springs from the floor to the table and up into the air, screeching a loud, angry battle cry. "Caw!"

Bert, his wings now spread wide, clamps onto the side of Number One's head. The force built up by the speed of his jump snaps the man's head to the side and sends him crashing to the floor with Bert still clinging on. I look away when he screams and the wet sound of tearing flesh start to mingle. Underneath me, Number Two tries to sit up, and I throw another strike at his head. I'm off balance, and only catch him with a glancing blow, but it's enough to push him back to the floor. I scramble on top again, regaining my leverage, and lash out with another more-solid blow. Yup. I've definitely broken something. On the plus side, Number Two is dribbling blood from between split lips, so I'm pretty sure that I'm winning.

"Search complete," the room speakers say, and I realise that the smoke has cleared and the screaming has stopped.

"Summarise details," I growl, keeping my attention on Paloma Number Two. "Were either Gary Locke or Carl Sanders logged in at the same time as Edward Redwood?"

"Subject Carl Sanders's log-on time is...fifteen minutes prior to Edward Redwood's log-on time. Virtual Monitoring files confirm that subjects Carl Sanders and Edward Redwood met during session. Do you require further detail?"

"No." I narrow my eyes. "Bert. Drag him around."

"Caw," Bert replies, and hops off Paloma Number One. He brings the body around, and I force the bile back down my throat.

I grab Paloma Number Two's hair and twist his head around as awkwardly as I can manage. What can I say? My hand hurts, and I'm blaming him. That, and I want to make it clear that I'm in control here. He raises his gaze to the shredded mess that used to be his partner's face and cries out.

"Who hired you?" I yell over him.

"Dean...Dean Hollister," he shouts.

I tighten my grip on his hair and crash my other fist into his cheek. "Try again."

"Crazy fucking bitch," he sobs.

"Bert," I say, and the shiny little murder machine walks slowly towards Paloma Number Two.

"I swear," he whimpers. "He said his name was Dean Hollister."

I nod to Bert, and he stops, staring menacingly at Number Two. "What did he look like?"

"What?"

I lift his head up and slam it back down into the floor, then repeat myself through gritted teeth. "What. Did. He. Look. Like?"

"I don't know," he babbles. "Sorta floppy hair, I guess? It was in a virtual world server. He coulda used a filter to look different. Uh, he talked funny, all stuttery and shit."

I unclench my jaw and groan inwardly. Filters get picked up quickly these days, so someone wanting to do something in secret wouldn't bother to use one and would more likely just go with the scanned appearance that the better log-in chairs take. Addicts with homebrew equipment have to build the image themselves, and they tend to get monitored a lot more closely than clearly scanned people. Audio masks are monitored even closer, so I'm certain that this can only be one person: Gary Locke. I knew that there was something off about him.

I snap Paloma Number Two's head back towards me. "Did he hire anyone else?"

"No."

"Don't lie to me."

"No, he didn't hire anyone else, not from the boss man, definitely. He just told us where the cash was and logged off."

I tighten my grip. "Was I the only target?"

"Yes, just you." I narrow my eyes at him, and he starts to panic. "Okay, okay," he moans. "There was some Tech Shifter chick on Forster Street."

"He wanted her dead?" I ask, and smack him again.

"Stop fucking hitting me," he cries, and tries to spit out a tooth. The broken lump of bloodied white only makes it halfway down his chin. "I'm talking, okay? He wanted to kill her himself. We were just there to play transport for the body once he'd finished."

"Diu," I roar. "When did he hire you?"

"Like, an hour ago."

"Bert. One caw for yes, two for no, understand?"

"Caw, caw."

"Real funny, Bert. While you were running surveillance, did the target mention the name, Lori Redwood?"

"Caw."

"I am such an idiot," I groan. "I should've let her come back here. Bert, were you able to record what was said?"

"Caw."

"Computer, synch audio system to my phone and dial contact Lori Redwood."

Silence, then, "Synch complete." A series of melodious beeps ring out over the room speakers. *Ring-ring. Ring-ring. Ring-ring.* "The person you are calling is unavailable. If you wish to leave a message, please press one, otherwise, please try again later."

"Computer, hang up. Bert, did you record any data relating to virtual world sessions that the target entered during the last two hours?"

Bert goes silent, then replies. "Caw."

"Last question. Have you been recording everything since you came back home, including this conversation?"

"Caw."

"Good. When the police get here, I want you to play a message for me. Caw to start recording insert file."

"Caw."

"Hoove, you better be there listening to this. Bert here's got recordings of everything that's happened since he got back. Ask nicely, and he'll play them. I'll explain the rest later. If you need me, check the top drawer of my filing cabinet and look up the name Gary Locke. End message."

I push myself to my feet. "Hey, Paloma. I'm gonna go arrest the guy that hired you. When the police get here, you're gonna tell them everything. And I mean everything. Where you met him, what he hired you to do, how much you charged, and where he left the money for you. Everything. If you try to run, Bert here's gonna cut your Achilles' tendons. If that doesn't stop you, he'll go for the arms too."

"I ain't running, but I ain't telling the cops anything either. If that thing's been recording," he says, nodding weakly towards Bert, "then that's all you're getting outta me."

I grab him by the vest top and haul him across the room until he's sitting against the kitchen counter. I couldn't do it off my own back, but he's being compliant despite his refusal to talk, and so he kinda threw himself across the room for me. He probably just doesn't want to get hit again.

I nod back over my shoulder in the direction of the dead body by the doorway. "You see your buddy there? If you don't talk, Bert's gonna keep you alive, but make you look worse than that." I turn to Bert and add, "Slowly."

"Caw," Bert replies.

I don't wait for a response from Paloma. I just walk calmly towards the bedroom, kicking the discarded gun over towards Bert as I go. There's broken glass everywhere. That's gonna be a nightmare to get off the bed. It's not as bad as the blood soaking into the floor out in the office, though. Still, I can't complain too much. He would have headed back here the second he got the automatic signal that the door security had been compromised, so he made pretty good time. But I do wonder why he always goes for windows.

I reach under the pillow and pull out my Glock Vintage. It's designed to look and handle like the classic Glock 23, but with all the expected modern conveniences that come with firearms these days; it's got a lightweight but tough shell, should be impossible to jam, and it's set to incorporate multiple different bullet tips. A lot of people in the underground use "quarters", a nasty little flat point with a sharp, cross-shaped tip at the end. I prefer the older style, modified round-pointed .40 Smith and Wesson rounds, just like the FBI and IRS use. In part that's because I do like the cliché PI look. If people look at you and their inbuilt imaging kicks in, they'll start to treat you according to what they've seen on TV. All that means is they'll be more likely to miss it when you start doing things differently from what they expect, 'cause in their mind you can't possibly act any other way. That's a useful trick to have in your arsenal if you're up against the right sort of people. Mostly, though, I use these bullets 'cause, if given the choice, I'd pick the "shoot first and ask questions later" approach over the "shoot first and wish that you *could* still ask questions" effect that the newer style rounds tend to have.

I check the magazine out of habit, but I already know that it's full. Since acquiring Bert, I haven't really needed to carry a gun with me anymore. With my shiny little friend staying behind, for now, going old-school seems sensible. Just 'cause some idiots who consider themselves killers don't think Gary hired anyone else, doesn't mean that he didn't.

"Computer," I say. "The police should be on their way here already after the explosion. Put a message through to Captain Hoover for me. Use bullet points as follows. One, explosion was at Caz's office. Two, Paloma Brothers responsible. Three, one dead. Four, ask Bert. Five...Eddie Redwood was *not* murdered."

"Understood," the speakers reply.

I grab the side holster from the wardrobe and strap it to my belt while I walk back through the mess in the main room. Paloma Number Two is being very quiet now, and is keeping his attention on Bert, who has taken up residence on the chest of Paloma Number One. I make a point of not staring at Bert's handiwork, instead walking slowly out the door with my gaze dead ahead. I run the moment I hit the hall.

Twenty-Five

I SPRINT THE two blocks to Morton Heights and make a beeline for the elevator. My gun is clearly on display, so the complete lack of a security guard this time is a nice spot of luck for me. Once I'm in the elevator, I hit the button for floor three and finish completing the last of my warrants using the audio tool on my phone. I normally prefer to do this manually, if for no other reason than that it avoids people listening in, but speed is important right now. That it'll need an upgrade to allow me to make an arrest is neither here or there. Once he sees what's happened, Hoove will push it through, I'm sure.

Once I hit floor three, I run again, rounding corners until I can see the door to Gary's apartment. "Screw knocking," I grunt, and launch immediately into a series of hard kicks.

Crack. Crack. The middle lock snaps away from the frame, and I move my aim to the bottom end of the door. *Crack.* There goes the bottom lock. I step back, duck my head, and charge shoulder-first into the thankfully not reinforced door, ripping the last lock away as I barrel into the hallway. Slowing to a walk, I draw my Glock with one hand and hold my phone out with the other, the warrant clearly displayed on its screen.

"Mr. Locke!" I yell. "Mr. Locke!"

"There is no need to shout, M-Miss Tam," he replies from somewhere in the open-plan room at the end of the hall. "I have been expecting you."

I move carefully into the room and spot Gary Locke sitting casually in his log-in chair. Keeping my gun raised, I swing my body from side to side to check that no one else is tucked away in the back of the room, and once I'm satisfied that we're alone, I hold out the phone towards Gary.

"Gary Locke. I have a warrant for your arrest, under the charge of conspiracy to murder. As far as I'm concerned, you can shove your rights up your ass."

"Language, M-Miss Tam," he wheezes, grinning like a guy who thinks he holds all the cards. "When th-the Paloma Brothers did not come back, I thought that you may drop by. I had not realised that they would use explosives. I had requested discretion."

"Then you should have hired a pro," I spit.

"Ah, but until Eddie's will is read, my funds are limited."

"That and you had to work quickly, right? The files I got from Hollister were infected with a copy of Eddie's modified SnapDragon tool, weren't they?"

Gary smiles arrogantly and nods.

"No wonder the damn thing was running so slow. What did it send you?"

"Copies of the files, and details of your searches."

"Internal or external?"

"Both."

"Yeah, well, you're not the only one who can get inside information. One of the idiots you hired told me that you intend to kill Lori. Where is she?"

"Right now? I could not honestly say."

I can hear the sirens in the distance now. There's no way they'd have come here yet, which means that they're just arriving at my block. Now I understand why he could hear the explosion; the walls are ridiculously thin. On the plus side, the recordings that Bert took here should be nice and clear. Something still feels wrong, though. Maybe it would be better to stall until Hoover and the boys come busting in. Or I could drag him outside and haul his ass back to my office to save them the bother.

Yeah, let's do that.

Gary nods at a point over my shoulder, and I turn without thinking. A rock-solid fist connects with the side of my head. My legs go numb, and I drop to one knee, my phone flying out of my hand and crashing hard against the wall. On instinct, I tighten my grip on the Glock and try to raise it towards whoever hit me, but my vision is too blurry. A hand closes tightly around my fingers and twists, causing me to drop the gun, then slams into my chest, knocking me back.

"Did you bring her?" Gary asks, but he sounds miles away. The guy that hit me grunts, and a shadow moves across my line of sight, disappearing back towards the door. It reappears again shortly after, dragging something with it. The whole room looks like it's spinning to the side, but keeps jolting back to the middle again whenever it gets close to the edge of my vision. My stomach lurches, and I throw myself forward, forcing my hands into the floor as hard as I can to keep myself from keeling over while I retch. Somewhere at the other end of the room, I can hear Gary laugh. The sound of his arrogant chuckling pounds against my head more than my own hacking and coughing right now. He'll pay for that.

"Ah," Gary sighs, and leans forward in his chair. The bigger shadow hands something to Gary, and he tips it up over the pile on the floor. It must be a glass or something. The lump coughs and jolts upright.

"What...where am...Gaz?" asks a familiar voice, and I realise what had felt wrong. The Palomas were going to help dispose of the body, *not* transport the living person to Gary's apartment.

"Shit..." I grunt, and the Lori shadow turns towards me.

"Cassie?" She turns towards the big mass standing between us, then back to Gary and his chair. "I don't understand..." My vision clears enough to see Lori slump, her head bowed. "So it was you," she says, her voice a sad whisper. "You hired the guy that killed Eddie."

"Me?" Gary laughs. "M-Miss Tam, did you finish looking at the bank statements that you procured from M-Mr. Hollister?"

"Yeah," I say, the word burning in my throat.

"And did he p-pay Devin Carmichael to kill Eddie?"

"The money went from his account to Devin's," I reply. I can see straight now, but if I can keep my speech slow, I may be able to avoid taking another hit just yet. Letting my gaze flick to the side, I notice that the big guy responsible for grounding me is a hefty expressionless slab of suit and muscles. A hired bodyguard? No. Gary's funds are low. He said that himself. Someone after the same thing that Gary is, maybe? There's something vaguely familiar about the guy, but I can't place it.

"So Hollister did it," Lori says, her attention on me. She turns her head sharply towards Gary and tries to get her thoughts out, but she's still groggy. That'll be the combination of the shock of what's happening and whatever the big guy used to subdue her. I can feel the swelling on my own face, but there are no physical marks on her, so I can be pretty sure that he didn't hit her. "But how did you know...were you both...why?"

"Hollister didn't know that he'd paid Devin," I mumble. "Gary knew, but he wasn't responsible for the money transfer either."

"Then who?" Lori asks me, her voice pleading now.

"The IP address for the payment origin came up as belonging to 17 Cornick Crescent."

Lori's eyes go wide. "But that's…"

"Eddie was a believer," Gary says. "Some things he could see as useful to society, but extreme body modification?" He shakes his head, that predatory smile slipping comfortably over his face. "Tech Shifting, he said, was the beginning of the end of days. We were c-corrupting God's creations and spawning our own abominations. When *you* spent y-your grandparents' money on joining the flock of the fallen…" He pauses and smiles cruelly. "Well, that was more than he could handle. His dear s-sweet sister that he loved so much. Lost forever."

Gary leans forward and wipes a tear from Lori's cheek with a shaky finger, his other arm straining to hold the crutch in place and keep him upright. "You were already such a disappointment to him, what with your refusal to f-follow God's teachings and find a n-nice husband to settle down with. Did you know that he spent his evenings praying for your salvation? He hoped that you would rejoin the flock one day. All you needed was to meet the right man, he used to say. When you chose to start Tech Shifting, it made him feel like he had failed. Failed as a b-big brother, and failed as a believer."

"He wouldn't…he never…" Lori whimpers.

"Wouldn't he?" Gary laughs, forcing a coughing fit back down just as it begins. "Poor Eddie felt that he no longer deserved to see heaven, such were his failings, so he chose suicide as his punishment. In his eyes, his failure to keep you s-safe, Lori, cost him his soul."

Lori is shaking, unable to even try to respond now. I step in, attempting to give her a chance to recover. "Then why do it like this?" I ask. "Why frame Hollister? Why not take his bullshit reasons and throw himself under a bus?"

"M-my father is a lawyer. He is close to M-Mr. Hollister and helps negotiate the deals for his products with the military. I too am a believer, M-Miss Tam. A believer in peace. Peace without the need for force. To learn that m-my father was involved with strengthening what is nothing more than a legalised band of thugs was a shock. I tried to convince him to stop taking jobs like that, but he refused. The money was too good, he said." Gary lets out a short bitter laugh, and spits, "So I left home and never looked back. When Eddie told me about his troubles, I saw an opportunity.

"Religion is sometimes as destructive as our armed forces, but the true believers can be useful tools in the war for peace. I offered him an olive branch, you see. 'Use your death to bring down the man responsible for y-your sister's fall from grace,' I told him. 'It could be your salvation, your redemption. And maybe w-when Hollister is exposed for what he is, your d-dear Lori will see the error of her ways. Save *her,*' I said. 'Even if you can't save yourself.'"

Gary turns back to the shivering Lori and smiles that awful smile again. "Your brother's feelings were pure, and his beliefs heartfelt. That made him easy to manipulate. But do not misunderstand me. Eddie truly was a friend to me. For that reason, I wanted to see him find peace. I wanted to help him. And, if in doing so, I could cause one of the biggest contributors to army resources to fall, then all the better."

"But it didn't work," Lori whispers, barely finding her voice. "The police thought that it was an overdose, not murder."

I pick myself up into a sitting position but make sure to let myself slump back again, struggling to ignore the smell of the chunk-filled puddle in front of me. "That was the point, wasn't it? You were banking on Lori chasing this. Once someone uncovered Devin Carmichael's involvement, you knew that the police would be told to back off. This isn't just about the army; you want to bring down the local PD too."

"The police are as corrupt as any businessman," the big guy replies. "They pick and choose who gets sent to jail and who gets to walk away. They deserve to have their secrets uncovered."

Sounds like someone has a chip on their shoulder. Maybe he lost a friend or a relative to someone the PD couldn't touch? He hasn't lost my Glock, though. I can see it peeking out of the top of his trousers. I just need to find a way to get to it.

"So are you a contributor on *The Roots of Eden are Rotten*?" I ask.

"Yes," Gary replies, his eyes glowing with pride.

I shake my head and try to make a wound. "You could proclaim Eddie's death a murder, pin it on Hollister, and even blame police incompetence, but no one's going to take it seriously if you post it on *that* blog. And the press? Anyone who does a little digging will see that the transaction took place in Eddie's home. The only internet access he had was through his log-in chair, and that was locked to his retinal scan, so it'll be pretty obvious that Hollister couldn't have done it."

"You underestimate us, M-Miss Tam. The headset will unlock automatically tomorrow. At the same time, Eddie's program will destroy the meeting audio files and overwrite the transcripts. The changes will be subtle, but just enough to add to the guilt. That includes both his copies, and yours. After that, all of M-Mr. Hollister's dirty little secrets will come out."

"But that won't work now. If you kill us, things will start pointing to you. If you don't, then you know that we'll tell everyone. Either way, you lose." The wild look in Gary's eyes catches my attention and I realise the mistake that I've made. "You never intended to get away with it, any of it, did you?"

Gary laughs, the sound catching in his throat and sending him into a coughing fit. He struggles to get himself under control, but eventually forces the last hacking cough out and relaxes back into his chair a little more.

"Of course not. Ah. Eddie, now he believed that we would. He was very confident in his work, you see, and deservedly so, but he didn't stop to think about how M-Mr. Hollister would defend himself."

"He already knew how to trace the program," I reply, and give my head a wary shake, blurring my vision slightly. "He'd be able to prove that it existed, who created it, and what it was doing."

"He knew how to trace *part* of it, yes, but he would be able to find the rest easily enough. Then, he would need to grant an external body access to his systems in order to verify his claims."

"But then they'd know what had been falsified," Lori says. "Everything you've done would have been for nothing."

"There's no smoke without fire," I say, glancing over to Lori. "Even if the files are proven to be edited, there are plenty of people who would believe Hollister did whatever Gary wants to pin on him, purely by virtue of the case coming to light. With Hollister's standing in the business world, there'd be no way to prevent it going public." I turn to Gary and add, "That's not enough, though, is it? You think that he really is hiding something."

"Oh, I know that he is," Gary rasps.

"I don't understand," Lori replies.

"Any investigation would have to be pretty in-depth," I say, keeping my attention on Gary. "They'll go through the non-edited stuff to search for signs of tampering and to get a comparison for signs that other files have been tampered with. Every secret Hollister has will become known to the team assigned to the case." Gary flashes his teeth, and I turn back to Lori. "Even if he's not directly under investigation for wrongdoing, the moment the PD turn up anything untoward in Hollister's systems, they'll turn it into a double investigation. The key was giving them a chance to find the files themselves. If Gary just handed over a bunch of stuff that he'd stolen using the program, they'd simply arrest him for hacking without even checking the files."

"But you'll be sent down now too," Lori says, giving Gary a look of pure shock. "You won't be able to see it all through."

"Even that has a purpose. What little I knew of M-Mr. Hollister's crimes, I learned from listening in on m-my father's telephone calls. His inadvertent breach of confidentiality, combined with the scandal of my actions, will ruin him and force him out of his immoral business."

"You want to save him. Like Eddie wanted to save me?" Lori tries, and Gary shakes his head.

"No, I will destroy both of them. And by falling while doing so, I will become a-a martyr for those like me who wish to instigate change in this world." He pauses and closes his eyes with a sigh. "Ah, but I will not be the only casualty in this war." Gary nods to the big guy and says, "Get the bag."

Mr. Suit and Muscles walks to the hall and hauls a large black sports bag into the room. Gary's avoided using this guy's name. That has to be intentional. Maybe he's gonna leave before the police arrive, then play the concerned neighbour or something like that once Gary's in court?

The nameless muscle drops the bag to the floor with a muffled *thunk*. He unzips the bag and throws a familiar-looking Lycra suit at Lori. Next, he removes the three pieces of metal that form Ink.

"Get changed," Gary says. When Lori doesn't move, he says, "We can make you watch while we kill M-Miss Tam, if you wish? Or we can hurt you. Maybe even both. Change now and I can promise you that this will be quicker than if you don't."

Lori starts to sob, but does what Gary says. She moves herself to the corner of the room, and starts to peel her clothes off. Thankfully, neither Gary nor the other guy complain when she turns to face the corner and hide herself as best as she can. As soon as she has the bodysuit on, she takes the metal spine and whips it over her shoulder, but it takes three attempts to get it to take to the plugs. Once it locks into place, the top tube opens out, snapping closed around her body. She flips the mask down herself, then works her way first into the back legs, then the front legs.

"Now come here," Gary rasps.

It's strange, but seeing her creep across the floor the way she is, I can tell that this isn't really Ink. When I saw her in the suit before, Ink had a natural feeling of strength and confidence that Lori only shows in flashes. At the same time, this isn't Lori either. Even at her lowest points over the last few days, she's never looked so defeated. Everything about her body language says that's she's given up.

"If she bites," Gary says, addressing the big guy but keeping his attention on Lori, "shoot her." He leans over and slides a small box out from the side of his chair. "I have a habit of stockpiling my stimulants. Did you know that the lubricating oil you have to put in the Tech Shifter suits also contains a small trace of certain strains? They are modified, of course, but they help with the immersion, or so I hear."

"What are you doing?" I ask, just as the sirens start to sound outside. Better late than never, I guess.

Gary opens the box and pulls out a syringe. "You were wrong, M-Miss Tam. My plan was never reliant o-on Lori taking action. If anything, her doing so was a problem. For things to work as I wished, I needed control over the proceedings. You both becoming involved added an unknown element into the mix. One that could cause things to happen quicker than was convenient. I also did not anticipate M-Mr. Hollister being as open as the transcript of your meeting indicates." Gary coughs loudly and forces a deep breath in. "Ah, but then without that..."

Gary looks down at Lori, his eyes a mix of pity and determination. "M-Mr. Hollister's openness was truly inspirational. I t-trust, Lori, that you feel guilt over what happened to y-your brother, yes? Believer or not, you must atone for your sins. You are going to overdose, just like Eddie. It seems only fair, wouldn't you agree?"

Gary unsheathes the needle in his hand and studies the contents. "You, M-Miss Tam, as you might have gathered, were to die in a hit ordered and paid for by M-Mr. Hollister. Now, you will simply die here. Perhaps I will be able to claim it was self-defence, hmm?" He glances up at the big guy again, nods towards me, and says, "You may kill her now."

The man takes a step towards me, his hand going to my Glock. I wait for the tip of the barrel to be showing, then push myself to my feet, swinging an uppercut at his jaw. It causes him to stumble but doesn't drop him. I snatch at my gun, ripping it roughly from his hands, and unload three rounds into his chest. I swing the gun around before he hits the floor, and fire a shot into Gary's leg. He cries out in pain and drops the syringe to the floor. From the way he'd been gripping Lori's masked face, I'd guess that he'd intended to inject the stimulant directly into her eye.

Gary leans forward, pressing one hand tightly to the bullet wound, and grabs at the syringe again with the other hand. This time, I step forward and kick him hard in the face. He slumps back into the log-in chair, his nose a bloody mess and his breathing coming through in rasps.

I hear the thunder of footsteps coming up the hall. The cavalry is here.

Within seconds, Captain Hoover and three armed cops storm into the room. I let my shoulders sag and begin to relax, but Lori panics and tears from the room.

One of the armed men turns to give chase, and I say, "Let her go for now."

The man looks at Hoove, who nods and turns to me. "Lori Redwood?"

"Yeah," I say, and slump into one of the armchairs.

Twenty-Six

SITTING HERE READING the first news report to cover the conclusion of the trial, it's easy to say that the days following Gary Locke's arrest went by quickly. They felt like they dragged at the time though.

After I gave Hoove a rundown of what had been said, he got straight onto the phone to Inspector Bergesson and explained the mess that he'd been landed in. As our dear Captain brazenly told his superior, simply leaving this one alone was no longer an option. If the postings queued up on *The Roots of Eden are Rotten* were allowed to go live, then it wouldn't be long until the public became aware of the harmonious working relationship that the local PD has with Devin Carmichael. The calls for action would be too much to ignore and that would mean they'd not only have to bring Devin in—and good luck with that—but that they'd have to haul every senior official in the PD through the mud in the resulting investigation. Rather than deal with such an inconvenience, Inspector Bergesson immediately authorised a site hack by the Data Monitoring Office. The account was frozen, the posts were copied and deleted, and I was dragged into the station to run through possible solutions to the problem of what to do with Gary Locke as a result.

Sometimes, good people can do bad things and still be good people after the act. I never believed that back in Vancouver. That was why things ended the way that they did. Would I be any different if I hadn't left home? I doubt it. My father's death shook me up, and if the right circumstances had come up, I'd have strayed from the path that I thought I was on. It took coming here for me to realise that there never was a straight and narrow path to begin with. It was New Hopeland that showed me I wasn't a paragon of virtue, and that I was, in the end, no different from anyone else. So, embracing my doing-bad-things-for-the-greater-good side, I called Dean Hollister. I explained how I'd obtained his bank details and what I'd discovered. I explained what Eddie and

Gary's plan had been, and I explained what I thought would be the best way to make this all disappear.

To his credit, Hollister was happy to let my shenanigans with his bank statements slide as it essentially cleared his name. It took two days for the Data Monitoring Office to cobble together a program to trace the alterations that Eddie's tool had made to Hollister's records. In that respect, having his log-in chair set to unlock itself was the dumbest thing that Eddie could have done. Once we had the physical proof of what he had planned and what had actually happened, we hit the point where I expected resistance from Hollister. My view was that if we dug up the original intent and reopened the Redwood case, then the stuff that came out would mean Gary gets what he wants. That would have been the right thing to do, regardless of the result, but we didn't have the luxury of doing the right thing. Life in New Hopeland isn't perfect, but it works. If we wanted to make sure that it kept working, then we had no choice but to do the wrong thing, at least to a degree. To my surprise, Hollister agreed, which made me wonder just how many pies he really did have his fingers in.

The result of our scheming was that Hollister agreed not to pursue legal action against me for my actions, and most importantly, he agreed to make a full statement confirming that he would not be pursuing any charges against Eddie Redwood, Gary Locke, or *The Roots of Eden are Rotten*. By then invoking his constitutional right to privacy, it became impossible to mention the particulars of his involvement unless the police thought it relevant to the case that they *were* going to pursue. The charges raised against Gary Locke needed to be specific for that to work. We settled on kidnapping and attempted murder. With Lori not answering her phone or her door, we were a little shaky on the kidnap part of things. What saved us on that point was the DNA on the clothes that Lori had left in the building, and the match that the forensic team found on both Gary and his cohort. This was confirmed as a match for Lori by using her hospital records. The charge of attempted murder was easier. Aside from my own testimony, Gary was so convinced that he'd won that he was happy to confess to his plan to kill both me and Lori. By doing so, he was eliminating those who sought to maintain the broken society in which we lived, and he was ensuring that the corrupt were exposed for all to see. Or so he claimed.

I paid a visit to Devin shortly after we finalised things with Hollister, and let him know what had happened and that he wasn't going to be dragged into it. Being in the business that he is, he already knew. I asked if he'd told me that he wouldn't name a price to kill the guy who hired him because he already knew that it was a suicide. Apparently, he did. He'd worked with Hollister before, recently as it happened, so knew that the voice at the other end of the phone wasn't his.

"Ya see, darlin'," he said, "Hollister's generally a good guy. He ain't got enough skeletons in the closet for me to turn him down for work, but he's got just enough that I'm not too worried if someone's trying to mess him around. 'Sides, any fool could've traced the payment and seen who made the transfer. The truth would've gotten out one way or another. You just made the experience all the more exciting for the public."

I called him a *ham gaa caan* and walked away. I should have probably called Charlie too, but like Devin, she keeps her ear to the ground enough to know what was happening. While I was motivated by the curiosity of whether or not Devin knew who had hired him, I didn't have anything like that with Charlie, so stuck to avoiding her.

The case was rushed to court after less than a week, the system allowing it to be expedited due to the seriousness of the crime. No charges were levied on me for killing the man who kidnapped Lori for two reasons. One, it was clear from both my own and Gary Locke's statements that I was acting in self-defence. Two, Bert's recordings caught Gary ordering him to retrieve Lori. This helped prove that my client was in immediate danger, and as a licensed investigator, I have dispensation to apply certain levels of force in order to protect a client in these circumstances. As it turned out, the man was named Michael Vesper, and he looked familiar because he was the security guard I'd thought was ignoring us when Lori and I first visited Gary.

With the original case falling under a gagging order due to Hollister's input, Gary found himself removed from court shortly after he started ranting and raving about Eddie Redwood. This, as it turned out, was part of Gary's state-appointed lawyer's plan of attack.

"Gary Locke," he said, "clearly suffers from a clinical fanaticism, and this has seeped into his perception of the everyday world in which we live. As a result of both this and his sad addiction to synthetic stimulants, he is incapable of making the rational choices that are expected of most citizens. Gary Locke accepts responsibility for his actions, his statement makes that clear, but he is incapable of understanding the weight of them."

Long story short, the final result was exactly what the news sites are now reporting. Gary Locke attempted murder and got rewarded with a private cell and a whole load of psychiatric treatment at public expense. What the reporters don't know is that we ultimately achieved our goal here: he got jail time, and he didn't get to deliver his message of rebellion. That, at least, is a job well done.

Twenty-Seven

IT'S BEEN OVER a week since the Paloma Brothers broke in, and I'm still a little jumpy every time that I hear a knock at the door. But hey, I made the news, so anyone who comes knocking should be expecting me to welcome them with a gun, right? Judging by the look on Plain Jane's face when I shove the door open and swing my Glock out towards her head, I seem to be the only one thinking that.

I drop the gun back to the holster, and wave her in. "Jane, right?"

"Well, hello to you too," she replies, breezing in through the door. She takes a quick look around and makes a beeline for my couch. "I hope you don't mind me dropping by. Tobi gave me your address. He said that you helped him with that trouble he had with his bank account. Exes, right? Always trouble." She sits herself down with far more elegance than I usually manage, and looks over towards the small metal beastie that's just pulled itself up onto the armchair across from her.

"Bert, leave her alone," I say, and he moves from staring menacingly to staring slightly less menacingly. I pack some cups away into the cupboard and ask, "So what brings *you* here?"

"Lori." Jane sighs.

"I haven't seen her since the night we arrested Gary Locke."

"*I* have."

I look over my shoulder at Jane, and she holds up a pair of house keys, jangling them lightly. Bert tracks the movement but obviously decides that they really are keys and not some sort of secret mini-bomb. He's been really twitchy since that night too.

"I tried her at home. She wasn't answering."

Jane drops her hand, and there is concern on her face. "She *can't* answer right now. She hasn't come out of Ink yet."

I turn around and cross my arms. Including the night she ran off, that's nine days she's been wearing the suit, assuming that she hasn't been taking it off for periods between visits. Even then, that can't be healthy.

"That's a long time to be Tech Shifted."

"Yes, it is. You know, she called me that evening. She was feeling a bit low because you sent her away, or something like that. She told me about how you two were flirting. It's funny. When you turned up at the meet asking about her, I figured that you were some new lover. Then, when she wanted me to give you the door key, it kinda solidified that in my head. I was a little off the mark with that one, huh?" Jane laughs at herself, and continues, "Anyway, once she relaxed, she told me a little about what was going on, but didn't really give me much in the way of details. I think that she would have, but someone knocked at the door and she had to let me go. From the way her voice jumped, I think she was hoping that it was you, but I guess it was the guy that took her."

"I guess so." I sigh. "Look, Jane...Lori told me that when she's Ink, she's running from stuff. Trust me on this. After what happened, and what we found out..." I shake my head. "She has a lot to run from."

"I figured that much out myself. Right now, though, I'm pretty sure that she's only eating and drinking because I'm stopping by and leaving stuff in a bowl for her. She's retreated far enough that she's pretty much become a stray cat."

I turn away sharply and press my hands to the edge of the sink. I can feel myself blush again as I remember the last time that Lori had mentioned the word "stray", and the stupid question that I'd followed up with.

"I don't get what you're expecting me to do."

"For a detective, you're pretty bad at spotting the obvious, aren't you?" I look over my shoulder and glare at Jane, and she says, "Talk to her. I've tried, and she just won't snap out of it." She shakes her head sadly, and her voice drops. "She normally talks to me about everything. If she's this far gone...None of us want to lose her."

"If you're that close and she's not biting for you, then what makes you think that I'll be able to make a difference?"

"Because you were there. You know what caused all of this."

"That doesn't mean that I know how to fix it for her."

"No, but you could try."

"I tried calling her," I yell, my anger catching me off guard as I rail on her. "I tried stopping by her house. She clearly doesn't want to talk to me either. You coming up here, trying to tug at my heartstrings, doesn't change that." The look of shock on Jane's face extinguishes the flames enough for me to notice how heavy my breathing has gotten all of a sudden. I take a moment to compose myself, and mutter, "Sorry." I should say more, but hey, I've stopped speaking already, so why continue?

"You're really worried about her, aren't you?"

"After what she's been through? Of course I'm worried about her."

"No, I mean *really* worried about her. Like, really, *genuinely* worried about her."

"Yes, I'm genuinely worried about her. Why wouldn't I be?"

"It's just that...once I knew that you were sort of working for her, I kinda thought that...maybe...you flirting with Lori was just a way to keep a client on side?" I narrow my eyes and Jane splutters, "No, no, I mean, it wasn't anything that *you* did specifically. Lori just has a habit of getting taken for a ride, is all. She can be pretty naive at times, and part of me was just expecting to be helping her drown her sorrows right about now."

"You honestly thought I'd be that much of an asshole?"

"You wouldn't be the first she's taken a liking to. And besides, over the two times that I've met you, you've made insensitive comments that border on discrimination *and* yelled at me without provocation."

"Hey, I apologised both times," I remind her.

A cheeky grin grows on Jane's face and she replies, "Well, yeah. But if you have to apologise, all that means is that you did something wrong to begin with."

I roll my eyes and return the smile. "Maybe you just bring out that side of me?" Jane laughs, and I continue, "Seriously, though, I meant what I said. I've tried talking to her. She obviously doesn't want anything to do with me."

"Then try again. Make her talk if you have to."

"Make her?" I repeat, turning it into a question.

"Someone has to, and I don't know how."

I raise an eyebrow in suspicion. "And why exactly does 'someone have to' if she doesn't want to?"

Jane fixes me with a serious look and says, "Because right now, all she's doing is carrying out a long, painful suicide."

I blink. "Diu."

Twenty-Eight

I AGREE TO try speaking to Lori, and Jane jumps at the opportunity to give me a ride there. I can't see any reason to turn it down; it's quicker and cheaper than calling a cab, and I'm happy to mark it down as making up for her deciding that I was an asshole based on one meeting. Jane drives at a speed that would put Lori to shame, so we arrive at Foster Street in record time. I insist that she leaves me to speak to Lori alone, and she agrees as long as I try to give her an update as soon as possible.

And so, here I stand, in front of Lori's bungalow with a spare key in my hand, and her best friend's number in my cell phone.

I'm certain that Jane is right, though I doubt that she knows it. I'm pretty sure that she used the word "suicide" to create emphasis. Either that or it was the best comparison that she could come up with for what Lori is doing to herself. If Jane were there that night, she'd know why Lori is doing what she's doing. The thing is, Lori isn't stupid. She also clearly takes good care of both herself and of Ink, so she knows how the Tech Shift system works better than I do. If Jane hadn't explained it to me on the way over, I wouldn't have any idea how damaging it could be to stay shifted this long. Lori *must* know what effect this is having on her body.

I slide the key into the lock, turn it, and push the front door open. I make sure to close it again gently so that I don't spook Lori, then walk up the hallway and turn right, stepping into the living room. There, curled up on one cushion of the two-seater couch, just like Jane said she would be, I find Ink.

Lori peers out from behind the mask, and her gaze lingers on me for a moment. She looks beyond tired. I take a step towards the couch, and Ink stretches out, letting her body take over the other cushion. *This space is mine*, the movement says. *Keep away.*

"Cheeky little kitty right to the end, ain't ya?" I ask, rolling my eyes and stepping across to the armchair opposite Ink.

Lori watches me sit down, then looks away and closes her eyes. She lets out a quiet *huff*, readjusts her front legs, and ignores me.

"You do know how worried you've got people, right?" I try. "Jane came all the way to my place to give me a key and ask me to try talking to you, because she doesn't know what else to do."

No response.

"If you want to get picky, you still owe me five thousand too."

Still no response.

I groan and throw my head back, letting my gaze come to rest on the ceiling. That's a shockingly clean white. She must be a neat freak. I bet she rolls her toothpaste up at the bottom too.

"Come on, Lori, help me out here. In case you haven't noticed, I'm not very good at this stuff."

Again, nothing.

I drop my head back down and stare at Lori. "How long are you going to keep this up, huh?" My voice is low and tipped with more than a little annoyance. I spot Lori screw her eyes shut tighter. Hurrah for open curtains, clear skies, and a good angle on the sun. Fine, then. If that's what it takes to get a reaction, I can do angry just fine.

"Diu, Lori," I snap, and the floodgates open. "What happened to you was shitty, but do you have to keep moping like this? Do you really think that *this* is what your brother wanted?" Lori snaps her eyes open in shock, and I keep pressing. "Your brother was deluded, but he did what he did because he thought that you needed saving. And how are you repaying that? By locking yourself away and watching yourself die?"

Ink rises to her feet on the couch. She bares her teeth, and Lori stares out at me in a rage. I rise to my feet and growl, "You think you scare me, kitty? Huh? You want to know what Bert did that night? He ripped a man's face to shreds, right in front of me. You've got nothing on him. I tell you what, Lori. Your brother did something really stupid, but at least he only did it because he cared about you. He loved you right to the end, and if there really is a heaven up there, he's looking down on you now and he still loves you, even though you're acting like a fucking moron."

I hear something in the back of my head talking, but I'm too far gone to stop it spilling out now. When the words come, they drag the tears with them. "You want to know what's worse than having a brother who loves you die, Lori? Having a mother that's still alive, but that hates you now, will hate you tomorrow, and is still going to hate you when you eventually have to put her in the ground. No matter what he did, no matter what mistakes he made at the end, at least you know that you never screwed up enough to make him hate the fact that you're still alive. At least *he* never wanted to trade your life for someone else's."

Ink sits back on the couch again. The rage is gone from Lori's gaze now, replaced by a mix of surprise and concern. From somewhere in the mask, Lori asks, "What happened to you?"

I sit down again and say, "Come out of the suit and I'll tell you."

"Tell me, and I'll come out of the suit," she replies, her voice rattling around inside the metallic muzzle. When I don't immediately respond, she adds, "I promise. And if I don't, then...the instruction manual is hidden under a sliding board in the closet in my bedroom. That has the keyword you need for the emergency release on the suit."

"And now I know that, what's to stop me just going and getting that right now?"

"You won't do that," she says, and I can tell that she's sure she's right. "Because you'd rather that I made the decision myself."

So that's what it'll take, huh? *Well, that's just great, Cassie. Well done for starting this one.* I let out a long, deep sigh. "Fine. But you're getting the short version."

"Okay."

I groan. "My parents were both born in Vancouver. Mom was a full-blood native, but Dad's heritage goes back to Pok Liu, Hong Kong if you trace it back a few generations. He was a cop. A good one too. It's not as bad in Vancouver as it is here, but the police had their fair share of problems with corruption. Dad refused to play into it all. As far as he was concerned, it didn't matter if it hurt his career, as long as he did what he was meant to: uphold the law. I admired him for that. I mean, I loved my mom, but it was my dad that I most wanted to be like, so I signed up for the police academy the first chance I got." I shake my head. "That place was run by the wrong people. I made it clear that I was going to be like my dad, that I wouldn't be bought or bullied, and they found a way to kick me out. The funny thing was, I expected my parents to be disappointed with me, but they weren't. At all. Instead, we all sat down together and discussed what I could do.

"It was Dad who suggested that, if I really wanted to go into law enforcement, then maybe setting up as a PI was a good idea. He helped me get the licences, taught me how he worked, and started pushing cases my way. They were always the same sort of thing; small cases where the police wouldn't touch it for whatever reason, but that wouldn't ruffle too many feathers if I ended up solving them. He knew the limits, my dad. The problem was, I didn't.

"This lady came to my door one day, talking about how her daughter had been killed. The police had ruled it an accidental death, but she believed that it was murder, and that the person responsible may have been one of the senior members of the local government. When I spoke to my dad about it, he said that he wouldn't have sent her my way if she'd come across him first. He knew of the case, but he said that the person the investigation had been allocated to meant it was something that went deep. 'Cases like that,' he said, '*shouldn't* be the way they are. But they are, and there's nothing that you or I can do about that'. He looked really sad about that. Like he thought I'd think of less of him because there was something that he couldn't do.

"The idea that he was in the wrong never crossed my mind. I just treated it like any other case. Dad couldn't work it because his job had boundaries, but mine didn't. So I took it on, against his advice, and started digging. He found out, of course, and he tried to warn me off when word started to spread around the police station, but I wouldn't back down. This was *my* case, and I would not let myself be kept down like he was. He was worried. Really worried. So much so that Mom tried to get me drop it too, but I just kept going. It was seeing my dad feeling so low about not being able to touch it that drove me, I think. As far as I was concerned, he was my hero, and I hated knowing that he felt like he was letting anyone down."

I sigh. "The thing with digging is that if you do it long enough, the chances are you'll find something. And I did find something. Evidence. Evidence that the guy who my client suspected not only committed murder, but was also knee-deep in a lot of dodgy stuff that should have prevented him from holding office. So I gathered it all up, marched into the police station, and slammed it all down on the table, declaring that the police had to do something or I'd go to the press. The police acted, exactly as I'd hoped, and arrested the guy, but they released him on bail. I expected him to try to run, but he didn't. He decided that there was no escape for him, and so he may as well take *me* down with him.

"He was a licenced gun holder, but no one figured that it would be a good idea to remove his weapons after he was released on bail. Stupid, right? It was almost like the PD did it on purpose to make sure I wouldn't do something like that again. They were already on their way to our place when all hell broke loose, so I don't think that they expected things to go the way they did, but hey, they were bent cops, not fortune-tellers, right? Anyway, the guy broke in a little while after we'd all gone to bed. He found me, pulled his gun, and squeezed the trigger, one, two, three, four, five times," I say, miming the gunshots with my finger. "The next thing I knew, Dad was slumped in front of me. The guy raised the gun again, and Dad sprang up. He took another shot, but he still managed to disarm the guy. So then the police show up, and everything starts to blur together until we make it to the hospital."

I wipe my eyes and ask, "Do you know what the last thing my dad said to me was? He told me that he was proud of me. He said that he loved me, and that he was proud that I refused to back down, even when he couldn't do the same. Mom was never the same after he died, though. She wouldn't talk to me for the longest time, but I kept chipping away at her, trying to cheer her up or get her back on her feet. It turned out that I was the one keeping her down. When she did start talking to me again, she told me that constantly trying to get her to open up just reminded her why her husband was dead. Apparently, I just didn't know when to quit, and look where that got the two of us. Me fatherless, and her widowed. It didn't matter that Dad was proud of me when he went, because in that moment, she hated me. She hated me then, and she hates me now, because as far as she's concerned, I broke our perfect home.

"A couple of months of her constantly reminding me of how she felt about me was all that it took to get me to leave. I've not been back since. I don't call, I don't write, and she's no different. So, yeah. Eddie loved you, and it all came to an end. My mom hates me, and it just keeps going. I tell you what, though. If I had that time again, I'd still take the case, and I'd still dig until I hit gold, because knowing that my dad thought that I did the right thing when he couldn't was enough for me." I pause long enough to look up at Lori and drag a few stray hairs back behind my ears. "And that's all you're getting out of me."

Ink studies me, and it really does look more like Ink now. Her posture is more relaxed, and the way she's sitting is more naturally feline than the weird, disjointed stance that she's had since I got here.

She drops her head, and Lori's voice says, "I doubt the milk's still good, but if you don't mind it black, you're welcome to make yourself a tea or a coffee." Ink hops off the couch and skulks out of the room, and moments later there is the quiet *thud* of a door being pushed shut and the slightly muffled *click-click* of Lori unlocking Ink's front legs.

I slip my phone out of my pocket and fire off a quick text to Jane: *She's changing out of the suit now.* I'd give her more detail, but she was the one who sent me up here, so I'm placing the blame for me having to dig up crappy memories squarely on her shoulders for now. Besides, as messages go, it tells her what she needs to know.

The kitchen doesn't look too bad compared to what I was expecting. In fact, everything is pretty neat. But then, given both the abnormally clean sheen to the living room ceiling and that Jane has been visiting daily, I guess it makes sense. I fill the kettle and notice two bowls on the floor. The first is a silver dish half full of water. There's a small puddle around one side where some of it must have spilled. Next to this, a large black bowl with the name *Ink* embossed over the front and surrounded by a cutesy paw print pattern is full of half-eaten fries and an empty burger bun. That makes me smile because, way back in school, I had a friend who had a cat that she insisted would only eat fries.

Thinking on it, I wonder how it works for Lori to eat and drink when she's Ink? I know the muzzle isn't as long as Jane's husband Murphy's is when he's being an Alsatian, but it must be awkward. I suppose I could ask. She did say she liked that.

The boiler sitting at the back of the kitchen springs into life, filling the room with a low hum. Lori must be having a shower. I close my eyes and let the sound fill my head, and the darkness slowly fades into the image of water flowing from a shower head, soaking Lori's lightly toned body as she tries to wash away the memories of the last week and a half. I can see her tears mingling with the clean water, and I reach out to comfort her, to help her forget...

Squeak.

The image shatters, and the hum fades back in, followed quickly by the *click* of the kettle. I slowly open my eyes and look down. My foot is pressed firmly on top of a squeaky mouse toy the size of my hand. Its tail is attached to a thick string that trails back towards the side of the ground-level cupboards at the opposite side of the room, where it connects to a big red stick that appears to have fallen down out of its shadowy corner.

"I guess Jane was trying to coax her out with play," I say to myself. Huh. Now I wonder why my mind went there rather than asking something obvious like, "What's this doing here?" or "Since when could you get cat toys this big?"

I shake my head and head over to the fridge. Lori was right, the milk is chunky. I pour myself a mug of black coffee and prop the vile-smelling carton up in the sink, ready to be washed down once I know that Lori's out of the shower. A quick check of my phone shows that Jane wants me to ask Lori to call her when she feels up to it. Fair enough. I think I can pass that on without holding a grudge.

It takes another five minutes for the boiler to switch off, most of which time I spend staring at Mr. Squeak-On-A-Stick and wondering what other oversized toys she has. It isn't until I pour the milk down the sink and try to break up the lumps that I realise what I'm about to do.

When I'd gotten angry with Jane earlier, it was because I really did worry about Lori, and when she wouldn't answer my calls or open the door, it felt like I'd been rejected. The anger wasn't entirely aimed at Jane, or at Lori. It was more a case that, for the first time in longer than I can remember, I'd actually tried to make a connection with someone and felt that I'd somehow managed to screw it up. That anger was all for me. The anger with Lori when she was still dressed as Ink, though, that's all hers for being so stubborn that she made me dig into things I prefer to bury rather than deal with.

I hate to admit it, but I'm actually pretty nervous now. I started noticing photos appearing in Charlie's house about a year ago. They're mostly of her, smiling happily with someone else. I've been leaving it so long between visits that there always seems to be new ones each time that I drop by. I spotted the latest snap when I went to speak to her about Flash7 sales at the start of the case. It was taken at the local park, and was of just the girlfriend, sitting on a picnic blanket. She was laughing. I never begrudged Charlie moving on, and I still don't. I'm not jealous of whoever her new partner is for being with her. I'm jealous of Charlie because she's been able to step into something else, while I've been letting myself wallow. It would be unreasonable for me to expect her to refuse to date all the time that I'm single, but I hated that she didn't anyway. But then, she never mentioned the new partner when I did visit either. She always asks if I've met anyone, and I always dodge the question, so she probably avoids the subject in order that she won't hurt me. She's like that.

It's not as if no one's shown an interest in me over the last two years, but I've always sent them on their way with either a scowl or an insult. In some cases, both. There are always excuses that I can feed myself to justify my rejection of them; this person's got a reputation, that person's too forward, this one's just got one of those voices. The truth is that I don't want to get hurt. All those little walls, all built up to stop myself from ending up in the position where something important can just fall apart again...Yet here I am, peering over those self-same walls, knowing I'm about to try to do just that. I hated the feeling of being rejected by Lori, so now I know she didn't turn me down, I'm going to give her the chance to actually do it? I am such a masochist.

"Someone looks serious," Lori says.

I don't look up. "Dead milk. It makes me think about life, the universe, and everything."

"So is *this* what you normally wear?" she asks.

I'm currently in a pair of light blue sweatpants, faded white trainers, and a lightweight fitted T-shirt in a luminous pink tone that clashes horribly with both. Hardly glamorous, and a far cry from Lori's usual "rock" edge. It's honest, though, I guess.

"Only when I'm planning to go for a run," I reply, and turn to look at Lori. She's changed into a pair of boot-cut jeans and a loose-fitting black-and-red-striped jumper. It's hard to tell whether the style of the jumper is making her look smaller or she's lost weight over the last week and a half. "I let Jane know that you were changing out of Ink. She asked if you'd call her when you feel up to it."

Lori nods. "I was going to anyway. You know, if you want to talk..."

I hold my hand up, and Lori stops talking. "I don't want to talk, and I don't want pity. I wouldn't have brought any of it up at all if I didn't think that you needed a kick in the ass." I smile to show that I'm not angry, and Lori sighs in relief.

"I guess I was being pretty stupid, wasn't I?"

"Yeah, you were. But hey. You came out the other end. That's what matters."

"Seriously, though, Cassie, thank you. I wouldn't have..."

"Take me to dinner," I blurt, cutting over Lori mid-sentence.

"Sorry?" she responds, unable to keep the shock out of her voice.

"Take me to dinner," I repeat, and nod down to the food bowl. "You clearly haven't been eating properly, and I haven't eaten today either so…take me to dinner, and we'll forget about the other five thousand that you owe me."

Lori stares at me in disbelief, and a smile creeps up onto her face. She leans into the doorframe and tilts her head against the wood. "You know, you are absolutely adorable when you're flustered."

I can feel the blood rush to my cheeks. I want to say something back. Something funny or clever. But all I can do is stand here and stare like an idiot.

Lori laughs playfully and steps into the kitchen. She walks past me, and I'm certain that she's exaggerating the sway of her hips on purpose. "So where do you wanna go?" she asks, leaning over to pick up the giant mouse toy.

Twenty-Nine

STANDING HERE, REPLAYING it all in my head, I can remember it all so clearly.

The night went by quickly.

Neither of us really wanted to go anywhere too fancy, so we opted for Tourniquet, a late-night café tucked behind the northern end of Main Street. I hadn't heard of it, but Lori apparently likes to drop by every now and then and said that the food came highly recommended. It was surprisingly big; Lori explained that it had been built out of the remains of an alternative nightclub, and had retained a lot of the original clientele. What that meant was that the fancy black tables were all seating a mix of Tech Shifters, Metalheads, Retro Lifestylers, and a handful of the BDSM crowd, in full gear.

I did ask Lori if she picked this place because of familiarity to her or because she thought that it would make me feel uncomfortable. She just laughed and summoned a waiter. To her credit, she was right about the food. Even just the simple burger and fries that I ordered was immaculately prepared, and the beer seemed to be as never-ending as Lori's mineral water. That's one of the advantages of being a non-driver; in situations where I feel naturally out of my depth, such as first dates. I can ply myself with alcohol to loosen up.

The conversation was good and started with the usual stuff that you'd expect on a first date. For example, I learned that she's twenty-four and shares my taste in film, and she learned that I'm twenty-seven and like to occasionally mix my love of jazz with old Wildhearts and Shinedown tracks. The more the beer hit me, though, the more I began to yammer on about anything and everything. Nerves and alcohol are not always the best of bedfellows. For the most part, I don't think my behaviour was too bad, though a lot of my questions seemed to revolve around how Lori feels when she's Ink and why such and such person was wearing whatever strap of leather. By the end of it, I was flushing. I'm not exactly prudish, but Lori knows a lot more about the kink scene than I ever thought possible. Whether that's down to Lori being deeper into the scene than I thought or just my own naivety and lack of knowledge about such things remains to be seen.

But hey, she said she likes it when I ask questions, right? And it's not like I was the only one learning things that were potentially uncomfortable. At one point, I even managed to blurt out something about Jane mentioning Lori dating assholes in the past and immediately went off on some sort of rant about what had happened with Charlie and why I felt the way I did. It took right up until I'd finished talking to start panicking that I'd just made myself look like I was either desperate or on a multiyear rebound. Cue manic babbling and apologising from me, and fits of hysterics from Lori.

After the meal, we considered hitting a nightclub, but I was a little unsteady on my feet so we decided against it. As a result, we headed back to mine a little early. I asked Lori in, and she said no. The repressed emotional side of me sank a little then, but the cold, logical side reminded me that I'm too drunk to stand up without the assistance of my shiny new door and that is hardly the most appealing sight in the world, let alone one that's suited to dance floors or continued conversations. Lori having also had to half carry me the whole way probably didn't help either. So, rather than pursue such a lost cause, I asked outright if she wanted to see me again. That was when things got strange for me.

Of course she did, she said, but when depended on me. She told me that, as I'd shown such an interest in the nice people in Tourniquet and why they got their kicks the way they did, she was going to teach me a little about obedience and rewards. Of course, genuinely forcing someone to do something against their will went against the rules of the scene, so if I didn't want to play along, then she'd be happy to call me when I'm sober and arrange a date the old-fashioned way.

Right now, part of me thinks that I should have gone old-school, but so many things stopped me. For one, I didn't want to disappoint Lori at all, and I was worried that not playing along would have done just that after I'd spent the whole evening throwing out what were, when I look back on them, pretty invasive questions. Two, I really was interested in what she was going to have me do. Most importantly, though, I trusted Lori. After all the openness she showed at Tourniquet, I had a fair idea of how things worked, and I knew that she wouldn't try to push me into something that I wouldn't enjoy. So I asked what she wanted me to do to earn my second date.

"Tomorrow, you are going to take yourself to 16 Fenchurch Street, you are going to knock on the door, and you are going to talk to Charlie. You will tell her everything about why you've avoided visiting her, you will apologise for being so silly, and you will try to repair your friendship. If you want to talk about the awesome attractive younger lady that's made this all possible for you too, then you get bonus points." That was what she said, word for word.

I asked why she picked that task in particular, and she replied, "Because BDSM is based on trust, and trust goes two ways. In this case, you have to trust me not to make you do something that you don't want to, and I need to show you that I trust that what you told me was true and that you're not still interested in Charlie in the way you're interested in me. Plus, I don't want to see you isolating yourself, especially from someone that you seem to genuinely want to remain connected to. Whether you want to keep doing things like this is up to you, and if you decide that it's too much, you can say so at any time. So. Will you accept your task?"

My heart was pounding then, and I said that I'd play.

"Good," she replied, and kissed me. I expected something forceful, suffocating, but Lori was gentle. Our lips pressed together, parted slowly, and our tongues met, slipping softly over each other and twisting together in a tentative dance. And just like that, she pulled back, and it was over. "Good night, Cassie," she said, and then she left.

And so, here I am outside number 16 Fenchurch Street. I've been standing here far too long now, and probably look like some sort of weird stalker to the neighbours. I'll look worse to Charlie if she's noticed. I could call Lori, apologise, and say that I couldn't do it, but what would that prove? That I can face down people with guns but that I can't handle polite conversation? Okay, so that's sort of true, but I like my various pits of denial, so I'll just have to pretend I'm not that person.

I sigh and walk up the path to the door, give the bell a couple of rings, and step back. *Lori told me to knock, not to ring the bell. Does that count as a failure? Maybe I should turn back...No, now I'm just looking for excuses. Ugh. I hate being such a wuss.*

After a moment, the locks click and the door opens. "Caz?" Charlie says, not even attempting to hide her surprise.

"Hi, Charlie," I reply, confidently owning the short sentence of greeting. Unfortunately, I then immediately launch into a barely coherent babble. "So, I figured that it's been a while since I just dropped by, and since I don't have any work on at the moment and you're probably done with your dealing shift by now, I thought that..." I shake my head to clear away the panic, and try again. "Look, I've kinda wanted to come and catch up for a while, but I haven't because I'm a complete idiot. Do you mind if I come in?"

Charlie smiles softly, relief creasing the corners of her face, and her eyes take on a warm, welcoming glow. "Of course," she says, and steps to the side.

About the Author

Matt Doyle lives in the South East of England and shares his home with a wide variety of people and animals, as well as a fine selection of teas. He has spent his life chasing dreams, a habit which has seen him gain success in a great number of fields. To date, this has included spending ten years as a professional wrestler, completing a range of cosplay projects, and publishing multiple works of fiction.

These days, Matt can be found working on far too many novels at once, blogging about anime, comics, and games, and plotting and planning what other things he'll be doing to take up what little free time he has.

Facebook: http://fb.me/MattDoyleMedia
Twitter: @mattdoylemedia
Website: www.mattdoylemedia.com
Email: mattdoylemedia@hotmail.com